LOVE, LOSS, LIFE...

LOVE, LOSS, LIFE...

GONCA ALBAN

Matador
9 Priory Business Park,
Wistow Road, Kibworth Beauchamp,
Leicestershire. LE8 0RX
Tel: 0116 279 2299
Email: books@troubador.co.uk
Web: www.troubador.co.uk/matador
Twitter: @matadorbooks

ISBN 978 1785893 421

British Library Cataloguing in Publication Data.
A catalogue record for this book is available from the British Library.

Printed and bound in the UK by TJ International, Padstow, Cornwall
Typeset in 11pt Aldine401 BT by Troubador Publishing Ltd, Leicester, UK

Matador is an imprint of Troubador Publishing Ltd

MIX
Paper from
responsible sources
FSC
www.fsc.org
FSC® C013056

To my teachers

What we focus on, we feed, so whenever we have tension in our heart and we're focusing on it, we're not shifting or healing it, we're feeding it. Be aware of the tension, but don't get lost in it. Bring light in to the area from the outside, from others, from nature and the Divine.

We heal our wounds by becoming aware of them, bringing them to the surface and using outside elements to work their magic on our pains and doubts and support our natural healing process. Outside elements can be anything from our friends and loved ones, to the sight, sound, smell and feel of nature, to music and reading, to creating, painting, writing, walking or dancing.

We note the negative, allow it to rise to the surface and then bring in the positive. It's the positive that transforms the negative and there is positive all around us as long as we are open to it.

We are a combination of light and shadow and to deny the shadow is to deny half of our very beings. Shadow forced down, pushed out of sight, ignored, denied and fought against lies awake in darkness, feeding on our negative efforts against it and growing bigger and stronger daily.

Shadow that is accepted as an essential part of us, brought into light to be seen, becomes an essential part of the colourful, multi-dimensional mosaic that is us, bringing beauty and depth to our characters and lives.

We are all beings put together like a colourful mosaic, or a vibrant, multi-coloured silk scarf. Each one of us holds within ourselves many different characteristics, many emotions, at times conflicting and multi-coloured with areas of light and shade. It is our wealth of colour and the depth that is found in the play of light and shadow that makes us whole and beautiful. When we begin to get to know ourselves in all our layers and contradictions, when we begin to accept ourselves for all that we are and when we learn to love ourselves, wholly, then we grow, find peace and joy and shine our inner light outwards, warming those around us.

Waiting

It was a hot and dry morning. It was always hot and dry here. The wind raising its head at times, then dying down quietly and as suddenly as it had woken up. The wind did not upset her, it could not dampen her mood, she was used to it. At its fiercest it threw the sand and dust in her face, but she had learned early on in life how to protect herself against its impulsive outbursts. She had made her peace with the wind long ago. Her mother hated the wind, cursed it when she heard its tumultuous hissing and roaring, but Cara welcomed it. She thought it carried a message from nature, a reminder of nature's strength and humankind's smallness compared to it. The wind had a will and voice of its own. It was uncontrollable and wild. Cara wanted to feel that wild energy within her, sometimes she thought she was an incarnation of the wind. The galloping, fierce rush of the wind mirrored her inner turmoil closely. She fed on the wind's energy and wild nature, feeling alive whenever it came out to threaten their world.

There were many tales of the fierce anger of the wind, but she could not understand the tales. The wind was strong and humans and animals needed to respect its rhythms. But as long as they didn't try to defy its natural way of being and its supremacy over all else, then they could learn to protect themselves from its destruction and use its power to their benefit. If they could only get to know the wind as she did, it would not harm them. She knew when to stay in or take shelter, how to walk with it, how to cover her face against the defiant sand rising up and combining forces with the wind. The two, when they combined their efforts, were a formidable force.

The turning of the wind from cool to warm, due any day now, was the surest sign they were on their way. The village folk called them the riders. Even the riders, the strong, independent riders listened to the call of the wind and worked in harmony with it. At least she believed they did. They never arrived with cold, blistering winds, or when the air was calm. Their arrival was like clockwork, every year they rode in as the winds changed from cold to warm, from harsh to gentle, from destructive to energising.

The riders had come every single year without fail, for as long as she could remember. Always as the winds turned, they galloped through their lands. She wondered if they spent their lives galloping through lands and villages, passing each at an exact pre-determined time of the year. Perhaps they reached each village as soon as the wind turned for their part of the world. But then maybe hers was the only village they visited. The chosen one. That was hard for her to believe though, as what their village had to offer could not possibly be enough. They didn't have much, they were poor and Cara could not imagine every other village on earth being as poor and desolate. There must be plenty, ease and beauty elsewhere. The savage harsh land and weather made life hard enough as it was. And the riders took their boys, their crops, clothes, anything else they deemed worth taking, leaving the villagers worse off every time. How long could this possibly go on before they died of cold or hunger, before they could no longer grow crops or hunt, before disease ravaged them and left the village full of corpses?

The villagers never spoke about them, but she knew the riders were despised by them all, seen as thieves and rapist. No one dared voice their feelings. What could they do against them anyway? It was the way of the world. Anyone who ever spoke up against them or voiced their fear or their anger were only met by others' cold, stony stares. All of them suffered and each one believed their suffering to be greater than that felt by the others. Someone else voicing their pain was felt as an insult, an undermining of their own pain. It was not tolerated.

The riders only stayed in the village for a few hours, they

never lingered, they were efficient in the way they worked. Only a couple of hours and yet the destructive effect of their visits were felt through the rest of the year. Just as people were making amends, gradually putting back together their lives, mending the fragments broken and shattered by the riders' last visit, just as they began to get used to the results of the ravage they had caused the year before, just as they were starting to come to terms with loved ones that had been taken, goods stolen, prides lost, the winds turned once more. Every year, always, forever, and the village was taken over by that same feeling of nervous expectation. Unspoken fear visible in everyone's stance and eyes. The waiting had started once again. They were waiting for the riders' return. They were waiting with that hollow feeling in the pit of their stomachs. The knowledge that pain was coming for sure. The uncertainty of what form it would take this year. Who would be lost, what would be taken, who would be beaten or raped. Uncertainty as to the detail of the coming pain, but certainty that pain was to be had, like the certainty of death at the end of each life. Only the details, the form this pain and suffering would take, were clouded in mist. The existence of pain to come was as clear as broad daylight.

The riders took, they stole, not only their produce, the food they had grown and tended all year and that should be there for them for their sustenance through the harsh winter, but they also stole the young women, mostly virgins and the little boys, the healthy strong ones.

The young women they took with them on their horses. They used them for a year, for sex, for cleaning, for keeping home, if their roaming, gypsy ways could allow for such a description. Then they would either get rid of them, or return them to the village, used, traumatised, often silent, filled with fear, damaged beyond repair. Most of the women who survived the year with the riders never recovered. They remained isolated, ashamed, weak and sad. None ever spoke about their experiences. No one ever dared ask them for a description.

That year away remained shrouded in foggy, grey mist, as an untold story, an undescribed adventure. The fear real but not quite understood by any who had not themselves experienced it. A fear that spread like a contamination from those who had returned to all those who had not yet been taken, but lacking in any real clarity.

The boys did not return until much later, until they had grown older and stronger, until they were fully trained, until they had become riders themselves. They did not remember their past, their roots, or if they did, they had been taught well to keep silent, to numb any calling from their heart towards their birth place, any sympathy for those they were now harming, but had once belonged to. They had been taught how to forget their mothers, fathers and siblings. When they did return, it was not to return to the village, it was to raid it as one of them, as a rider. They rode with the rest of the riders, to steal, destroy, torture and rape. Mothers, recognising their long lost sons would sometimes cry out to them in despair, unable to hold themselves back. They never received recognition, and sometimes they were hit with a hard whip or stick in their back for making a scene. Hit by their own sons.

Cara's brother had been taken when he was only five. One of the riders had grabbed him and placed him on his saddle, in front of him. Joseph had not cried, but the fear was visible in his eyes. His eyes, wide open, staring, begging. But his mouth remained closed, his face held rigid, his shoulders frozen tight, thrust high and close in. He had been trained from birth to obey and fear the riders. No one ever spoke up against them, no one dared. As they rode through, all eyes were cast down, searching the dry, scorched earth for an answer, an answer that never came. Those downcast eyes that tried to hide the hate and fear burning inside of them, burning up their near dead soul, eating up any remaining hope flickering inside.

Cara knew her turn was to come. She was beautiful she was told. She had just that year come of age. Part of her wished to go unnoticed. She feared the riders, although somehow not

as much as some of the others. But another part of her was waiting. There was no avoiding her fate, so she might as well make the most of the experience. The riders held a fascination for her. She found them attractive in their wild ways. Wild like the wind, wild like her innermost soul, wild like she desired to be, like she felt inside. She could not allow her wild side to be seen in her village, the part of her that she had to squash and hide, the side of her that would not be accepted, that would be shunned by her own folk. She was curious about the riders. She wondered what they did through the rest of the year. What activities took up their time. Did they enjoy themselves? Were their hearts as wild as their ways? She wanted to watch them play and laugh. She wanted to hear their stories of different lands and alien landscapes.

Women who returned never talked about them and any sentence about the riders that circulated amongst the villagers was nothing other than speculation and gossip. Those who knew, did not share. It was only those who had no direct knowledge that spoke and opined.

Cara was young and full of life, with a vibrancy of nature that was unusual in her village. She knew she didn't fit in. She felt like a prisoner, squashed, limited in her movements, compressed in her heart. She yearned to be free. She had a natural energy and a deep curiosity for life and everything in it. She wanted to experience life, see new things, taste exotic tastes. She could not tap in to the fear she felt held all around her. She didn't feel a part of it. Her heart did not understand it. She wanted to know, to understand them and their ways. How did they live, why did they harm, who were they, where did they come from, what were they like, what did they eat, how did they speak, what, if anything at all, did they feel about the harm they caused, were they even aware of the extent and depth of it?

She had heard the rumours, horrible stories, she could hardly believe were true. She had heard that the women were taken turns on. That sometimes they might have to put up with three or more partners in one night. And if they put up a fight or did not please, they were beaten and treated worse than slaves. They had to cook and clean, pack and unpack, carry water, gather wood and serve. They had to gather whatever was to be found growing in the soil and prepare the cooking fires. They were never allowed near the little boys. Their names were hardly ever remembered, they were ordered around by nicknames given to them. Harsh, undermining names like freckeles, red-head, short, fat, slow, crooked, whatever caught the riders' fancy or drew their attention on first sight. She knew that by the end of the year, they had been so thoroughly used, that a pain accompanied them for the rest of their lives, as a reminder of their year of humiliation, like a stamp pressed into them by the riders, to burn on their bodies forever. No woman was ever kept for longer than a year, no woman was ever taken twice. Damaged goods, used and expired was what they were and under that stigma they lived out the rest of their lives. Humbled to stooping, pained beyond any chance of experiencing joy again, broken in spirit as in body. They hardly ever spoke after they were brought back. Either they never again cried, wearing on their face a marble expression devoid of emotion, with fear set into their lines, or they cried all the time, unable to pull themselves together, crying silently as they worked or in the quiet of the night, or in a little hidden corner. It was as though they were frozen in time, their bodies rigidified, their souls buried, lost forever.

Not all women were taken though. In this village, perhaps the only place in the world, ugliness or disability in a woman was considered a gift from God. Those were the ones men courted and married, those were the ones who bore children and kept homes. There's was the only adult normalcy to be seen, but even their 'normal' lives were muted by the dark, heavy energy of the village. A village so poor, so robbed and pained, full of people constantly struggling, always losing, had little cause for happiness.

Hers was a solemn village all in all, a nearly dry and dead

one. She yearned for other experiences. She yearned to hear uncontrolled laughter, watch lively dancing, see eyes shining with joy and passion. Here, all was too dead for her lively soul. So in her secret thoughts she wondered if perhaps the riders, as wild, savage and brutal as they might be, could offer her a fuller life and more valuable experience in one year than all the rest of her years in this village added together could bring her. She was ashamed to acknowledge her interest and curiosity even to herself, but a part of her yearned for the excitement, the unknown, the adventure. A part of her wanted to be taken, to be set free, to get away from this forsaken, frozen place. Just as another part of her dreaded it and was afraid.

Her thoughts were interrupted by her mother's call. Her stoutly, strong, solemn, hard mother. Her mother had spirit in her, that much was certain, but it was a dark, heavy, unhappy, bitter spirit. She wondered what her mother would have been like if she had not experienced so much fear, pain and grief in her life. Maybe she would have been joyful, maybe then she would have been capable of love and laughter. Or maybe not. She could not imagine her mother any other way than she was.

She quietly followed the call and entered a small room where her mother was brewing tea. The pungent, strong smell of the tea filled her nose and throat. The strong smell was everywhere, seeped into the walls. She wished there was some milk to use. But they had not had milk in the house for over a year now. There was simply not enough milk to go round in the whole of the village, only the children were given some and even they did not get enough. She was used to black tea, but she missed the taste and consistency of milk, the comforting, dense feeling it created in her mouth and the filling heaviness it left in her stomach. There were only a handful of goats left in the village, not nearly enough for a hundred mouths. And one of them was poorly and for sure the strongest one would be taken by the riders, leaving them with only three for the year to come... She wondered if she would still be there to experience it.

Her mother told her to help with the vegetables. They

needed to start preparation for dinner. She went over to the corner of the room and piled a few potatoes in her folded arm. She carried them over and let them drop on the table with a thump. She felt oddly excited, anxious in her heart. She wanted to run out and be alone. She felt like dancing and laughing, or perhaps screaming and crying. Which one was the more overwhelming desire she wasn't sure. There was so much turmoil within her, so many opposing passionate emotions competing with each other for supremacy. Her spirit felt squashed and yet excited at the same time. She pushed away any excitement in her spirit and did as she was told. Theirs was a village full of obeyers, quiet, solemn, incapable of a rebellious thought let alone action. They all obeyed someone or another, their parents, their masters, the riders. Life was based on quiet stubborn acquiescence. They obeyed in their quiet, resentful manner, eyes cast down, as if they were ashamed to exist, inwardly hating those they obeyed, blaming them for their hellish lives and hating themselves for obeying. She had learned to do the same, but her soul rebelled constantly.

The thump of the potatoes was as rebellious as she would ever dare to be. Her mother glanced up at her, raising one eyebrow. Even that small act, that small thump, as tiny an action as it was, merely a fraction of what she felt inside, had been too much for her mother. She wondered how she would react if a potato found its way across the room and smashed against the wall. She smiled imagining splattered potato across the wall and her mother's surprised look, eyebrow raised in her customary way. She imagined her mother would not react at all except for the raised eyebrow and the frosty stare. Her eyes would communicate to Cara all that needed to be said "Behave. Clean it up. And don't you ever flare up like that again"

Her mother said "come now Cara, you're letting your spirit ride off far ahead of you again, remember where you are and what your duty is". Her voice, like her bearing, demanded respect. Not because she was one of those women who somehow created awe and respect through their being and presence, but because respect was something her mother desired and if it didn't come naturally, she would force it out at all costs, through whatever means necessary. Her mother's voice was harsh and bossy. It held threat in its tones, 'do as I say, or else...' Cara wondered how come her mother could not understand that respect could not be beaten out of a person. It was a feeling that arose towards those who deserved it naturally, without the necessity for force. She looked down, only now did she notice she had been staring at the mud wall wistfully, picturing the potato smashed against it, seeing the mess it created and finding satisfaction in the loud crash it produced. Imagining it bursting, splitting into two before it fell to the ground with another loud thump. She set to peeling the potatoes, carefully putting aside the skin for soup.

She enjoyed chopping, it gave her a sense of satisfaction. As she worked away, she wondered whether there was something wrong with her. Why did she always dream of destruction, noise, breaking, cutting? Even her pleasant dreams involved noise and movement, dancing, running, shouting, singing. Why could she not be like the others, quiet, turned inwards, heavy, solid, slow, grounded, at peace. Or were they at peace? She did not like being so impatient, too quick to act and speak, too loud as she tended to be, preventing her from blending in to her surroundings and becoming less visible, more like a shadow that could move around without drawing attention to itself. And again the question rose in her, were they at peace really? Outwardly they were calm and quiet, but their eyes spoke of pain and dread and suffering. She did not see peace and serenity in their eyes.

She missed her little brother. He had been lively like her. He was stronger too, not crushed by the severity of their mother. He had life in him. She was sure he would thrive wherever he went, whatever his fate held for him.

She hoped they had some carrots too. She was so sick of

eating boiled potatoes and onions, some carrots would make all the difference. She looked up at her mother, preparing to ask, but her mother was sewing, the expression on her face grim and set, her mind busy in her own thoughts and Cara dared not interrupt.

She fetched a couple of onions, glancing around as she did so in the hope of catching a glimpse of another colour, the orange of a carrot maybe, or the light green of cabbage. She saw nothing and returned to the table without hope, clutching two onions.

She hated chopping onions, they burnt her eyes and blinded her. How much nicer to chop a carrot. She held her breath as she went to task, concentrating on the chopping completely. The faster she chopped, the less pain her eyes suffered. The less she thought and dwelled on what she could not understand, the faster time would pass. She knew her thoughts led her round in circles. She never seemed to get anywhere with them or understand any more than when she had first started. Everything remained a mystery, some untold story, misted, dark, incomprehensible to her inexperienced, naive self. The circles swirled in her mind round and round, tormenting her further, making her feel dizzy and confused.

The riders came the next day. The villagers were prepared in as far as any community can prepare for such an event. They had been waiting though, so mentally they were ready. There had been a sense of expectation for days. The sound of the riders' horses pounding the dry earth brought a numb, dull, muted sense of terror with it nonetheless. Unspoken, unvoiced terror, terror that simply was and they knew they could never describe it or act on it. It was a palpable existence, some kind of live spirit that they could feel all around them. The air tasted of fear, their ears rang with it. It was suffocating even when Cara stood outdoors with the wind raging, blowing everything in its path and gathering it all in its strong arms, clearing the space of everything except for this throbbing sense of fear, too strong and pervasive, too much a part of the land and its people for even the stong wind to be able to lift it. A sense of stagnation prevailing within the commotion, a muted end, somehow stronger and more dominant than all else.

She withdrew into the hut as she had been instructed. She turned her back to the door, squatted by the fire and got to work sewing. Her heart was pounding even louder than the horses' hooves clattering outside, or the wind blowing its final threat-laden warning. She was sure the whole village could hear her heart racing. And yet she was able to sit very still. "How do I manage?" she wondered. "How do I manage to contain my wild spirit so well in this still, solid outer former when I have not even the slightest bit of control over my thoughts. My body is like this piece of string. I can bend it, sew with it, use it. Yet my thoughts and feelings are like wild horses, galloping uncontrolled, full of vigour, energy and rebellion. Their direction unknown to all who see me, unknown mostly even to me, uncontrolled even by me. They must have a wisdom of their own, an unhindered free energy with a life separate from mine, sometimes running with me, by me, in me and sometimes against me. Oh to be able to know that wisdom they hold, to feel it fully, understand it and move with it. She wanted to run free with her thoughts, with her wild soul, yet she knew she had to control herself. She had been trained well in the art of control. She had grown up breathing in others' stagnation and immobility, feeling them force their inertia on her, suffocating her and teaching her in turn to suffocate her own spirit.

She felt like a criminal, a liar, walking around amongst all these people she loved, who held good thoughts and calm tempers. She felt she didn't belong amongst them, her nature was not like theirs, hers was a nature that needed constant restraint, overwhelming care, constant control. She had to hide her soul, deny her true nature and hope no one else noticed. She felt it was a sin, that her essential being was sinful, that she was wrong, something was wrong with her. Her inner world contrasted so starkly to the world around her. She must be wrong, yet her heart screamed out with anger at her confinement, her soul bound down, shackled, iron and steel binding its very essence to the earth and the fate of those around her. That very essence that was made to fly, was being forced to rot.

Sometimes she felt as if the others knew. Her mother knew, she was sure of that. She was sure that was the reason her mother didn't like her. Her mother cared for her sister differently. She wasn't as harsh and judging with her. And Cara knew that her mother had never been able to get over the loss of Joseph. She knew her heart ached for him still. There was an emptiness in her, created by his leaving, that could not be filled by Cara. She was the wild one, impulsive and passionate, qualities her mother despised. Even her sister could not fill the void. The good hearted angel was how her mother referred to her sister.

"I have a good heart" thought Cara. "Why can she not see

it? I love and care. Why does she label me as the devil?" She noticed the irritation in her legs. They were aching to move, to leap and run. Yet she could not. She had been ordered to stay in and that was what she had to do. "Why are my mind and heart racing instead of my legs? At least my legs could be put to some use." Her mind quickly returned to thoughts of her mother. "Why does she hate me so?" She had never understood and her heart could not accept her mother's dislike of her. She tried so hard to please. She obeyed as best she could. She cleaned, cooked, sewed. And yet no action of hers was ever worthwhile, nothing good she did was ever noticed. She only ever managed to attract criticism from her mother. What she did was never enough, or it was wrong, or done at the wrong time. There was always a reason for her mother to turn her anger on her.

Barely perceivable she thought "My legs, they were made to run far away from here", but then she squashed the thought fast. It was a sin to think so. She was lucky and she knew it. "I am blessed" she repeated to herself several times, hoping repeating it would make it true. "Thank God for all I have, but still, I wish I could run and release the throbbing in my body. It's so painful to have to hold it all in".

She could not concentrate on her sewing. She kept forgetting where she was and what she was doing. There was so much going on in her mind. So many thoughts were rushing by and swirling around so fast.

There was no way of hiding though. The riders went in all the homes, looked in all the corners. People had tried to hide goods or loved ones before, but they had always been found, no matter what genius ideas had been used. Any attempts had failed and severe punishment had followed. Beating and whipping so bad, people had cried out in pain and wanted to die for long after the beating had ended. Cara's mother had not attempted to hide Cara. Cara wondered if she simply was not worth the risk or the effort for her. She wondered if her mother would feel relief if she was taken away rather than pain or loss. Then the thought occurred to her that she might not feel anything at all. In fact, maybe she would not even notice her absence.

She noticed her hands were shaking. Premonition maybe. In her heart she knew. She knew it was her turn. She could feel the expectation in her heart, the alertness of her mind and body to all outside sound and movement. She checked herself. No, no fear, she was not afraid. She was anxious though, nervous. She tried to still her hands. She dropped her hands into her lap, watching them, trying in vain to steady them. "I have no control over my hands either, I can calm them no more than I can slow my heart down", she thought. She wished she could run outside and get it over and done with. Whatever was to happen, surely it would not, could not, be worse than waiting without knowing. She felt the empty, looming nothingness of ignorance spread, time creeping by so slowly.

All sounds merged into each other, the very near needle clashing sounds her mother was making and the distant sounds of the hooves and rough male voices. All noises had become one with the beating of her heart and the turmoil in her head. All she could feel was a need to scream, a desire to jump up and scream, and then run.

It all happened suddenly. The whole episode was over before she had realised it had started. For her everything went by so fast and in a whirlwind of blurry images. Each image changing and being replaced so quickly that all detail was lost on her. One moment she was sitting there, watching her hands shake and feeling her heart gallop, the next moment she was standing by her chair, with her sewing material strewn on the floor where she had dropped it in her haste. She had heard him come in and risen without thinking, impulsively she had turned to see the intruder. What she saw was a harsh, worn face, a strong, muscular body, wavy long dark hair, a tall proud man with no brutality, nor a smile playing on his lips. What caught her eyes and held them still was the expression in his eyes. His eyes were green, with specks of brown and gold in them. They twinkled slightly. His eyes were smiling, not with kindness, but with a sarcastic sense of humour, a defiance against the world and whomever may take it in to their heads to stand up to him. He could be brutal all right, Cara saw that, but he could be kind too. Was their wisdom in those eyes? A light that said I have seen, felt, thought and lived? Cara was mesmerised by his eyes. She thought the man standing in front of her was the most beautiful creature she had ever laid eyes on. She felt her breath stop, her body and mind stilling into a deep silence. Her whole soul was crying "you can take me, I'm yours". But her body did not move, nor her mouth speak.

He called out to one of his men in a dialect she did not understand. The man he called out to came in and as soon as he did, her sparkly eyed rider marched out. She was still following him with her gaze when she noticed the second rider had grabbed her arm and was pushing her with harsh force, brutality even, towards the door. She turned on him in anger and shook his hand off. She managed only because he was surprised and hadn't been expecting anything but blind, mute obedience. But her look was enough to tell him that she wouldn't be pushed and shoved, herded out like a goat. She walked out unaided with her head held high.

She looked around for her rider, but he was gone. The one by her side now flung himself up on his horse and grabbed her arm, pulling her up behind him in one harsh jerky movement. And there she was, clinging on to a rider, up on a high horse, looking down on the rest of the villagers from her new vantage point. The height of the horse, the warmth of the rider, the movement of the wind against her face gave her a sense of strength. The defiance in those first beautiful eyes she had seen and loved had rubbed off on her. She would not leave in shame, her head hanging low, afraid, embarrassed. She would leave with her head held high, her chin slightly lifted and her eyes shouting "don't you dare pity me, look at me, look at how high I sit, don't you dare pity me".

And off they rode, all of them. She saw the riders gather

together. Some of them had other girls around her age hanging on behind them. These girls were marble white, fear shining from their eyes. She felt anxious, excited, but not afraid. Why was she not afraid?

She saw a boy too. She knew him and liked his mother, a kindly woman. He looked so young and fragile. She thought of Joseph. What had become of him? Would she be able to see him? Would they let her hold him? He was probably too big for that now. Was he happy? Had he grown strong? Would he recognise her? Would she recognise him? "Of course I will. I'd recognise him anywhere, even twenty years from now" she thought.

Her heart was ablaze. She was excited. The wind was blowing her hair back. She felt wild and free. Truly free. Free in her heart and body. Free from all that had bound her down, limited her and trod on her. An unknown infinity was waiting for her, spreading out in front of her with every movement forward. Now her movements, the speed of the horse, the strength of the wind against her face and body matched the galloping of her heart. She was no longer fighting her spirit, she was riding with it. Her whole body felt alive and every cell vibrated in tune with every other cell.

"How funny", she thought, "I am now a slave, and yet I feel truly free for the first time in my life".

They arrived at a campsite. There were no houses, or bungalows, or shacks. Instead the valley was littered with large, wide, high, sturdy tents. They were supported with wooden pillars and tree trunks, some were built entirely around the trunk and branches of a tree. Cara liked the idea of living under a tree, surrounded by its growth, protected by its strength and solidity, merging her life with their earthy existence.

Once she had taken in her surroundings, she realised how much they fitted in with the riders' energy. She could no longer imagine them in any other setting and wondered at herself for having imagined them in stone or mud dwellings, thus creating barriers between themselves, rough and free as they were, and the wilderness itself. What she saw was perfect and right.

For some reason she had sometimes envisaged them living in a world full of luxury. Grand buildings with gardens perhaps. But she quickly realised that was just an image from some fairy tale. Scavenging horseback men would never keep palaces and roses. Nonetheless, the tents looked pretty majestic and strong, fit for warriors and roaming kings. They looked like they had been built for durability and some sense of basic comfort. At first she could not see inside any of them, so her ever wild imagination conjured up luxurious abodes in each one.

Most of them had colourful hangings fastened on to them. The hangings glittered in the sunlight and danced to the gentle breeze. Even these simple, useful decorations were more luxurious than anything she had ever seen before. She could see rugs on the ground peaking out from under the hangings and when one of the hangings was pulled aside by a rider entering a tent, she caught a glimpse of richly colourful blankets and throws. She thought she had even seen some cushions. She wondered if they were soft. She wondered if slaves were allowed to use them, to snuggle against their soft support. But even if the only time she ever touched them was to wash and clean them, she still felt excited imagining their soft feel on her hands and the feast her eyes would be having with all the bright colours and exotic designs.

The horse she was on halted abruptly. Her rider didn't even turn around to face her. Without looking at her he reached his arm back, lifted and then practically dropped her to the ground. His treatment of her didn't feel rough anymore though. It seemed purely efficient.

Another rider standing near a large tent strode forward and poked the girls closest to him in their backs, chests or legs. All the girls from her village had been deposited in front of this tent, near the entrance to the campsite. They were all poked eventually, all of them pushed in to the big tent in the centre of a clear open space. This was the riders' communal tent where meetings and gatherings took place.

There were many more girls inside. She recognised none of those. They came from other villages and looked so different to her eyes. She wondered where they came from and realised how little she knew about the world outside of her village and other people and cultures.

They smelled different, wore different garments and had their hair done differently. In her village the women always tied their hair up in a bun at the top of their heads using little sticks they had scraped clean and smooth. But some of these girls were so much more imaginative and artistic. Some had their hair in pony tails, tied up with colourful ribbons. Their dark hair swaying behind their heads like the tale of a well groomed horse. Some had them plaited from the scalp all the way down to the tips. Some had amazingly long hair and some wore theirs very short. Some had their hair tucked under scarves. Some used many colourful ribbons holding their hair in various shapes, parts braided, parts in little pony tails, parts curled back and fastened to their heads. Cara liked their style best. She loved the little bursts of colour contrasting sharply with the black hair they were mingled in with. The sight was striking, the colours giving the faces below them a vibrant, lively shine of their own.

Their clothes looked different too. Some of them wearing bold colours, reds, pinks, violets, greens, and so many more colours she could not even name. There were vibrant designs, odd cuts. Some had thick lace. Some were dressed in white. Some showed a lot of skin, some none at all. She felt ashamed of her cotton pyjamas, formed of two loose fitting garments, loose trousers and even looser blouse, both the same colour, or rather, no colour, just the bland natural colour of cotton, grey from dirt and looking tired and worn, dried mud around the lower legs and ankles. How odd that so many different people could suddenly be thrown into the same pot, where as a few hours before they had had no inkling of each others' existence.

"Here stand the people I will share the same fate with from now on, bound together for the rest of our lives by our common experience through one short year" she thought, all of them the riders' newly stolen slaves. With that thought she realised that hers wasn't the only village the riders ransacked and pillaged. Already one of her curiosities had been quelled.

She felt curious about these other girls. What did they think of the riders? Were their villages as sullen and mournful as hers? Were they as poor and destitute even? Some of them certainly didn't look that way. How could you make such beautiful garments and afford colourful ribbons if you were poor and why would you want to if you were unhappy? Their attire whispered to her of vibrant cultures, dances and singing, camaraderie amongst women as they prepared each others' hair and helped each other with the sewing of colourful, vibrant clothes. "Vibrant souls create imaginative, beautiful looks" she thought, "and depressed, mournful souls don't create anything at all" followed as she looked down at her plain, worn, unimaginative trousers.

She wondered if they had boys and young men in their villages to appreciate their beauty, or were they stolen from them also? They must be, but then who did they dress up for? What was the point? Their air of pride and confidence suggested they took pride in their looks and took care of themselves, for themselves, satisfying their own desires rather than aiming for outside appreciation. Cara could not help marvelling at them.

But in that large tent they all found themselves in, even these vibrant women were quiet. Even they looked afraid and unsure, faced with slavery and the unknown.

Where did they live anyway? How far away? What did they do to afford their colourful lives? How did they make their livings and pass their time? What did they grow and eat? What were their enjoyments? Were their communities as strict and unforgiving? Were their mothers as harsh as hers? Were their friends as sad? Did they even speak the same language as her? Would she be able to understand them if they told her? She wanted to run over to them straight away and get to know them. Her questions were burning her insides, but she could not. She wanted to feel some of their vibrancy, be near it, enjoy it, be part of it. But there was such a sense of restraint and need to obey orders and rules, a restraint drummed into her throughout her whole life, she did not dare move. Her mind demanded she be quiet and obedient. She felt she needed to wait and be told what to do.

There were four of them from her village. She could feel their presence. She could see their downcast eyes in her mind, although she had not dared look at them directly. She was afraid they would read the excitement in her eyes, while she read their terror and shame in theirs. She felt her feelings must be a great sin, another burn in her heart, she could not show it or ever tell of it. She was afraid of her own excitement, a feeling she knew had to be wrong, but was so real within her. She knew through experience and instinct that they were afraid and ashamed. How could she meet their eyes that were screaming of pain with her own, clear, questioning, interested ones.

She wanted to see her rider again, the one with twinkling, humorous eyes. She searched for him, scanning the tent, but she could not find him in the crowd. Most of the men had left them in the tent and gone off somewhere. There were only a few of them still near, standing guard. What a waste of energy and time. It was not like any of them could have run away even if they had found the courage to. They had no idea where they were, or which way to turn. She wondered again if she'd see her rider again.

One of the riders standing guard, the one who had pushed her into her current position was standing quite close to her. She started examining him, taking in his clothes, they were clean and sturdy, made for comfort and endurance, not for appearances. He wore sturdy, much used boots. A whip was hanging from one of his hands. "No humour in his eyes" she thought. He looked harsh. Not evil necessarily, but not one that would endure light heartedness or fun. He certainly would not have tolerated a remark or question from her, one of the new slaves. Any form of defiance would not have been tolerated either. She looked down at the ground again. The ground was broken and cracked from lack of water. The poor old earth, mistreated, unappreciated and forlorn more than all else, yet stronger than everything, ever enduring and everlasting, nourishing, life giving. "How odd", she thought, "we walk on it, never appreciating it, never thanking it, yet it continues to give, without question, without expectation of any return for its generosity".

She pressed her feet into the ground, trying to connect to its strength, support, endurance and suffering, trying to learn from it. But her attention was caught once again by the bright, colourful scarves and dresses of other women.

She was in her own world, trying to guess from their attire and attitudes, the message in their eyes and the way they held their heads which women belonged together, which came from the same villages and had been brought up under similar influences. And then she started watching some of them, the ones that caught her eye because of an inner confidence and strength they held and that shone outwards. It was visible in their quiet, tense faces. Cara compared their countenance to see if they shared other characteristics. Then she compared their looks to some who came across as weak and petrified, unable to keep themselves calm. What differentiated these women? Was it all hidden in their inner fabric, shining outwards? Or were their strength and confidence engrained in the shapes of their noses, their mouths, cheek bones, eyes? She looked around searching for any shared physical characteristics, and any that stood out through their uniqueness, trying to tie physical appearance in with inner nature. She examined the expressions of their mouths, the way they held their heads. She felt that the outer appearance of these women mirrored their inner characteristics, that outer looks are formed and changed as inner worlds are changed. She continued for a while lost in her analysis until she noticed a commotion.

A few of the men had entered the tent. They separated once inside, fanning out in all directions. Each one went over to a girl, grabbed her arm and led her away. The girls that were taken were then led on to different tents. She was led to a tent too, but by a rider she hadn't noticed before. She felt her heart sink. She knew it was an outside hope, an unlikely wish, but she realised as she was pulled away by this stranger that she had hoped her rider would be the one to take her away. He was the one she wanted.

Love

He came to her at last. She had been waiting, hoping, not daring to hope, fighting the expectation, and yet still waiting and hoping in spite of herself. And he did come, at last. She heard the flap of the tent lift and breathed in the scent of male that drifted in on the clear night air. She knew it was him, she felt his presence. She held her breath. Would he take her? She was afraid, afraid of the possibility of him taking her and afraid of the possibility of him leaving, not wanting her after all. She was afraid of her own feelings and excitements, afraid of her own potential to want, want so much something that it overwhelmed her and she knew she ought not. She feared her desire for something that she had been led to believe was unacceptable, wrong, immoral, bad. Yet she felt calm at the same time. Calm in her heart where she felt a sense that this was right. Her feelings were okay. How could something that felt so deeply right be wrong? She felt excited too somehow. Somewhere in her heart she knew the time had come and she did not want to fight her feelings. These feelings unknown to her till then, that led her towards joy and hope, they belonged to her, they brought her peace. His smell so near her felt like arriving home, a true home, so much more familiar and warm than the one she had come from. Her heart had found a place to rest.

She felt his strong grip on her wrist and then a sudden jerk. Before she knew it she was up and being pulled out of the tent by him. She followed quietly, struggling to keep up, struggling not to trip over, her heart beating too fast for her small rib cage. She felt alive, as if she could fly, but only with his hand holding her wrist tightly, only with his presence flushing through her whole excited, warm body. She no longer wanted any other existence or way of living. A life away from his strength and solidity would be a waste, a half-life, partially felt, lived out without true satisfaction. As long as she could smell him, hear him, feel him, she was alive and free, her body felt strong, she felt light and capable of any feat.

He pulled her past a few tents. She could not see much in the dark. Then he led her up a side path ascending a hill to their right. The ground was rocky, with weeds sprouting out all around. He was practically carrying her as she struggled to keep up with his long gate. And then suddenly he stopped. He let go of her hand and pushed her inside a tent. It was colder in there, lacking the proximity, breath and body heat of others, further removed from other tents, more isolated.

She stumbled forwards in the dark, her eyes not yet able to pick out any detail, but there was no time to anyway. He pushed her down, onto something soft and grappled with their clothes, efficiently, hastily, without pause. It was over before her brain had a chance to catch up. Next thing she knew, he was lying next to her on his back, not far, but not too close. She stared up at the roof of the tent, wondering why this act held so much fascination for everybody, this simple, brutal, fast, efficient act. She felt no joy or pain, just a numb curiosity. She did not understand. But somehow it didn't matter, she didn't need to understand. She thought "But I have him now. He has come to me" and with that thought, a faint smile on her lips, she fell asleep.

She learned after a while, how to play with him, please him and get pleasure out of him. She learned the contours of his body, the play of light and shadow on his skin, the folds of his clothes. She learned to read the depths of his eyes, the sparkling flicker that danced in their beautiful greens. She understood the intricacies of his lips, the different shapes they took according to his moods, the words they spoke without any sound having to leave them. When talking or silent, when active or still, his lips told her what was going on inside his mind. She learned to understand and interpret every twitch, half smile, laugh, tightness and every other accent they produced. His eyes expressed in advance what his mouth confirmed after. She felt she knew him and every day her love for him grew stronger. The more familiar he became, the closer she felt to him. His presence brought her joy. When he was away she missed him and days seemed to drag on, heavy with the weight of his absence, nights dragged by even more slowly than the days. Her whole life was a play of being with him and waiting for his return.

When he was with her, she always wanted him to stay longer, time passed too fast. Her days and nights took shape around his presence or absence. Her heart and mind moved and lived around his expressions, satisfaction and words.

She liked the twinkling in his eyes. They were like the smile of a star when they flashed, communicating amusement and happiness. She seemed to amuse him a lot. He laughed at her naivety, her mistakes, her fumbles. He twinkled at her courage and determination, her obstinacy, her energy. He smiled at her efforts at women's work and her playing at men's work when she could get away with it. He even liked it when she disobeyed, as long as she had a good reason. She was proud and would not tolerate bad treatment. She worked hard, but she felt that was her duty, she was used to it. She flared up at rough or unjust treatment. She would not play the role of a slave, even though she understood that was what she was there. But her soul rebelled against such a label, and her pride stood up defiant against anyone who attempted to treat her without respect. She might work like a slave, she might be a slave, but she would not be treated as one. She demanded consideration and respect and her demeanour and hard work gave her the right to make such a demand. He understood her nature and grew to respect her. Over time his treatment of her became warmer and more appreciative. He felt comfortable in her presence and their treatment of each other was kind and familiar. She felt certain her feelings for him were reciprocated.

She learned to feel his approach, before she even saw him

or heard his steps. She knew his favourite foods, could feel his moods in his being before she saw his eyes, could pick out his voice from among all the other men, even when they were out riding in the woods nearby. She could feel it in her heart when they were returning from a trip, she didn't know how, but she always knew and had everything prepared for him the way he liked it. Making him happy and comfortable gave her more joy than any she had experienced before. His presence filled her heart.

She was happy, wrapped up and warm in his presence, excited with every day and night. She learned to laugh and smile, to wake up with expectation and joy and rest her head at the end of the day with contentment and gratitude. She felt alive for the first time in her life. She felt she belonged to this odd place, where it was she had no idea, but she felt she belonged in his tent, by his side. And she felt she would always belong to him, with him, by him, wherever he might be.

Sometimes she could not believe the depth and size of her joy, it was so much. She was surprised she could contain such magnitude of feeling, she who had never dared feel before. She could not believe how much life there was in the world. She found so much outside of her village, much more than she could have ever imagined. Even after a few days, she felt herself lose touch with the sadness and lifelessness of the village she had come from. How had the vibrancy of the outside world remained shut away from the cold death of her village? She had no idea. She did know though that her whole being was full of life now and she loved it. She wished she could pass some of her love and joy into the hearts of her villagers, fill them up with some of the vibrancy and passion of life she felt, so that they too could be happy, they too could love and dance, sing and run, and enjoy the world's treasures.

Could these riders, these men amongst whom she now felt she belonged have caused her folk so much harm to deaden their hearts? It could not be. Her mind could not allow it, could not grasp it. All she knew for the moment was that she lived, fully, joyfully. Her village must have been cursed long before the riders arrived. Her folk must be carrying a different death over themselves. She could not bring their depression and the riders together in her mind. She could not connect the two, or place blame on those amongst whom she had at long last found a sense of belonging and peace.

As days went by she grew more accustomed to their ways and their dialect. She felt a part of their community, of their lives. For the first time in her life she felt she belonged somewhere and more importantly, with someone. She kept his place for him, cooked his food and gave him pleasure. In return he made her happy just by being present, by her side. When he was away for a few days, she felt herself become listless, until his return drew near, when she came alive again. She would then busy herself making sure everything was ready for him, excited and full of expectation.

She sometimes came across the other girls when she was running errands around the settlement. She was allowed to move about freely and was making friends amongst the inhabitants. When she saw one of the girls, at first she used to smile at her, hoping for an exchange. She wanted to share her happiness with someone and find out what they were experiencing, feeling and learning. But the girls she smiled at stared back at her with distaste, sometimes anger and hatred showing in their eyes. Then they turned away. So she stopped trying to reach them. She was not one of them, she could feel that. She could not understand why they hated her so much, but she felt it had to do with her joy, with the way she lived her life with passion and interest and enjoyed her time and experiences, while they watched on, slowly dying inside, turning dry and bitter. At first she wished she could pass on to them some of the beauty in her life, give them a taste of what could be, reach them, touch their hearts with hers and help them out of their gloom and bitterness. "All they need is someone to help them see from a different perspective and feel the awe of life" she thought. But after a few attempts she gave up. They were not open to the exchange. They did not want it and they did not welcome her attempts. In fact they shunned her and avoided her.

Gradually she got to know some of the men and women who were part of the tribe. They were more open to her. Some of the men always stayed behind, to guard and protect those that remained and to do work around the campsite. There were also three women who were part of the tribe and remained with them year after year. They were not one of the girls, who were all returned to their villages at the end of a year. They were old and wise, called on for healing and spiritual advice. They were respected by the riders and held important positions within the community. They influenced decisions and were consulted regularly on important matters.

Two of them prepared medicine from plants and trees and tended to the ill or wounded. She had cut her leg once and been taken to one of them, whom they called Lobsang, meaning noble minded. She was given this name because the riders thought she created magic with her hands, preparing mixtures and remedies and healing all kinds of wounds and illnesses. They believed that such magic could only come from the gods and the gods would only give such powers to someone pure of heart and of noble mind. Gods could only perform through someone who was noble and pure in thoughts and actions. Anyone lower would pollute the healing and not be able to cure. She purely transmitted God's healing through her hands to the people. They believed she could not err and had complete faith in her abilities.

The concoction Lobsang spread on Cara's leg hurt worse than the cut, but it worked. Already the next day the wound was closing up and was visibly much better. Lobsang did not smile at her, not even once. When Cara asked her what the mixture was, she did not answer. When Cara smiled, she was ignored, a cold blank glare holding her smile for a moment and then dropping it like heavy lead. Lobsang's eyes were set hard in her face, no expression escaped them. Cara wondered what her story was and decided to ask someone else to tell her of it. She fascinated Cara, her roughness, the lack of expression, the harsh throaty grunts. She was interested, curious, but she felt no warmth in her presence, just awe and a slight fear. She wondered how such a noble mind could work together with a cold heart. How the holder of healing hands, working miracles through touch, could keep herself so distant at the same time.

Her favourite of the three wise women, the crones, was the one who read the stars and people's palms. She was called Tenzin, the holder of teachings. She was always consulted before important decisions or big events. Every new born was taken to her, so that the baby's life could be charted, its fate understood. The riders believed that if they knew a baby's fate, its natural characteristics and the forces that would work on its life and influence its directions, then they could better decide how to bring it up and how to focus its training. They would know its inclinations, they could strengthen its weaknesses and build on areas of strength. She was highly respected and her advice followed in every detail. She read the seasons and the moon. She understood people's characters, fears, hopes and dreams. She could see their unconscious and hear their prayers, spoken in the stillness of night without sound.

Cara first came across her when she walked out into the opening one night to look up at the stars and breathe in the night air. Tenzin was already standing there, looking up also, smiling up at the stars. Cara thought she must be speaking to them somehow. Tenzin caught her watching and smiled at Cara. Cara's heart filled with warmth. She felt that Tenzin's smile flowed directly from the warmth of her heart and connected to hers. Tenzin had softer features than the other two. There were lines around her mouth and eyes that told the story of a woman who was generally happy, someone who smiled often and who found amusement and pleasure in life. Her eyes were deep with wisdom, warmly welcoming and friendly.

Cara walked over to her slowly, her eyes still held by

Tenzin's. She wanted to talk to her, learn from her wisdom and spend time with her, absorbing her warm energy and learning from her wisdom and nature. But as soon as she reached her side, she realised she had nothing to say. She felt immature and silly standing next to this old wise woman. She was afraid of making a fool of herself. So she kept her mouth shut. Tenzin looked back up at the stars and Cara followed her gaze.

After a while Tenzin spoke. It was as if she was speaking gently to the stars, but Cara felt her words were directed at her. Her voice was softer than the other two as were her facial features and her eyes. More attune with milk and cream rather than with worn out rocks or thistles. "The stars smile at us, Cara, they bring good tidings, we will have much to be grateful for over the next few months"

"How do you know me?" she was so surprised Tenzin knew her name, the question burst out before she had time to think of something suitably intelligent to say. She blushed.

But Tenzin ignored her sudden outburst and said "You are a curious girl child and a fast learner. We will start tomorrow"

Cara was confused. What were they going to start? Had she missed something? She looked up at Tenzin with confusion, her brows knitted, her face puzzled.

Tenzin smiled again "The language of the stars, child. I will start teaching you what your heart yearns to know. You must be committed, listen, feel, think and understand. Above all, you must keep your heart and mind open, ready to take in what comes your way. You will enjoy it, don't you worry"

Cara was too surprised and overwhelmed with joy to answer. She looked into Tenzin's eyes, her own eager eyes telling Tenzin all the answer that was needed, although she doubted Tenzin needed any answer from her at all. She seemed to know everything anyway. Grateful warm tears started to flow, some faltering, many brimming over the edges, giving her eyes a joyful sparkle, the bright shine of excitement.

She stood there long after Tenzin had left. Her heart was

beating fast. She felt like jumping up in the air, a cry of victory shattering the stillness of the night sky. But she held still, holding her excitement, her energy and joy all within her rib cage. She wondered why she was being rewarded so. What had she done to deserve such incredible gifts and a life filling fast with wonder and joy.

She could not sleep that night, excitement carrying her well into the next day.

Cara was a fast learner and she had an insatiable appetite for new information. She was interested in everything and the more she learned, the larger her field of interest grew. Everything felt brand new to her. Every bit of new information she received, every new experience was exciting. With her growing interests and knowledge, her zest for life kept growing also. Her view of the world was expanding. The world started to take on the appearance of a vast playground. Her life felt like an exciting adventure with limitless potential.

Tenzin taught her how to look at the stars, how to hear their messages, appreciate their stories, tell their myths and how to read their patterns. Cara realised over time that the stars were a vast treasure chest, full of knowledge. People could learn so much about the universe and their place in it from these bright jewels of the sky. Their twinkle, their location in the sky, their movements , their relationships with other stars, all told those who could understand their language so much. The relationship of the moon to the sun and the stars, the positioning of the stars compared to each other and the sun, the shape and size of the moon, the constellations, the myths that went with them, in fact everything about the sky was full of wisdom.

Tenzin also showed Cara how to read the messages carried in the wind. She taught her how to predict natural events by feeling the moisture in the air, receive news from the songs sung by birds, analyse the movements and droppings of animals and how all of these seemingly banal, natural occurrences influenced human lives directly, how they affected their feelings, thoughts and tempers.

Different plants held different benefits and needed to be prepared in their own unique ways. Everything in nature had its own way of affecting human nature, even plants and foods. People's physical and mental health, their moods and their energy, their actions, thoughts and feelings were all influenced by the nature that surrounded them. Everything in nature, on earth and in the skies above, contained messages within them for people to learn from. Messages sent to support humans in their development, understanding and well being.

Tenzin had a wisdom and deep intuition of her own, born of long years on earth watching, learning, listening, feeling, understanding people and helping them. She knew why someone looked tired or sad, why another was restless and another quiet. She knew how to help them, what to offer and when to hold back. She read their thoughts, even with her eyes closed. She felt approaching news before it was uttered and foretold natural occurrences before they became obvious to the rest of them.

Cara respected her, but even more strong than that, she felt love for her. Cara's joy in learning was unleashed. Her sense of belonging full and her hunger for warmth, human contact and appreciation satiated. Her world was now complete. Her rider filled her heart and Tenzin her mind. They both taught her so much about herself. She felt blessed, with so much to live for and so much to enjoy. She avoided thinking about the end of her year. She could not, would not think about leaving. This was her life, a life full of happiness, learning, growth, satisfaction and beauty, more than she could have ever imagined or dreamed of.

Every morning she got up early, always full of energy, the rising sun stirring up excitement within her. She greeted the beginning of a fresh new day with a smile, watching the sun as it rose from behind the hills. She hurried through her morning duties with enthusiasm and abundant energy. And as soon as she had finished these, she ran to Tenzin to sit at her feet while they both sewed, listening to her stories, learning from her wisdom. She accompanied her on her walks around the settlement, helping and supporting people, listening to them and giving advice. She grew accustomed to Tenzin's melodic voice. She was careful to pay attention to what Tenzin held back from them and how much she told them. Cara always stood a little aside, remaining silent, listening and watching. She watched Tenzin's actions and responses, learning from these as much as she learned from her words and explanations.

Tenzin was kind and compassionate. She had a kind word and a warm gesture for everyone. She helped people, even when they had not asked for it. Sometimes they had not even realised they needed any help. She had a subtle, humble way about her, but if the situation needed it, could be assertive and strict too, still keeping a degree of warmth and caring in her interactions. She was able to quieten souls and ease minds with gentle words and encouragement. She was also able, without hurting prides, to coerce people into making changes or obeying her demands.

Everywhere she went, she was greeted with gratitude and respect. Groups hushed when she neared them, eyes looked up with expectation into her wrinkled, smiling face. Cara loved to walk by her. She enjoyed helping her help others. It gave her a sense of usefulness and that in turn increased her self-confidence. She never bore of watching and listening to her. Cara was a warm, loving person and at such a happy time of her life she had even more love to spread around than ever before. With Tenzin she had found a way to express her love and warmth without needing to hold back. The community first got used to seeing Cara next to Tenzin, then over time they grew to like and respect her too. Cara felt this was the best way to live, she felt she had found her calling at last, a home, a community and a purpose based on serving those she cared about. She could not imagine a better way possible to serve the universe and show her gratitude.

As she kept learning about nature and others, her understanding of herself grew simultaneously. She understood her own nature and moods better. She felt when her moods were out of harmony and could figure out why they were so and how to bring them back in to balance. She gained a better understanding over her, until then overly passionate feelings and racing thoughts, both of which had been a mystery to her previously. Her thoughts were no longer alien wild horses galloping off uncontrollably. They had a logic to their direction and a reason for their excitement. The more Cara understood them, the better she was able to work with them rather than trying to subdue them with force. She realised the beauty in all different moods and the preciousness of her own thoughts and feelings and their semi-free, wild style. She came to know them as friends and developed an understanding of them, through them of herself, and with them of others. She learned to be at peace with herself.

There were still times when she struggled and fought with her feelings or tried to shut down her thoughts, when she tried to change the natural flow of her inner workings, but these moments were getting less frequent. Her passionate, loving heart felt like a hurricane mostly, vast, strong, fierce, but no longer something to be feared. She could flow with it now. She was alive, able to contain her mad heart and share its warmth constructively. It no longer beat against her. Rather, its beat gave her life and rhythm.

He was away for a couple of weeks when she first started feeling sick in the mornings. At first she thought it was something she had eaten, but when it continued for a few days she went to see one of the older women who took care of their wellbeing. Lobsang was not there, so it was the other healer, Tsewang, who saw her.

The woman was wrinkled all over, bent double, as if the many years she had spent on earth were an invisible burden she carried on her shoulders, stuck there, heavy to bear. She seemed too old to still be functioning. Watching her Cara wondered how she continued to get through her days, the whole world a dead weight, crushing down on her fragile body. Yet functioning she was. Like someone speaking in dialect or with a strong accent, fluent, capable of communicating their thoughts and feelings perfectly, yet the foreign intonation obvious, Tsewang worked and lived as others, without problems, but with the dialect of someone who had seen, suffered and lived too much, for too long.

Cara walked in quietly, afraid to disturb the hush that seemed to descend on the world as soon as she walked in to this Crone's abode. Tsewang's back was turned on her. Cara wondered if she'd even heard her come in. Cara was about to clear her throat and say something, but before she could, the Crone turned around slowly.

Cara was struck by the Crone's eyes. Her eyes were clear blue and large and Cara felt like she was casting a spell on her. Her chest tightened, as if wanting to protect her heart. She didn't feel Tsewang was dangerous or could possibly mean to harm her. She looked kind, although distant in some way, but Cara was afraid of her piercing looks anyhow. She was afraid of being read. She felt the piercing stare cut straight through her defences, her mind, her thoughts, dreams and fears. She felt she had no protection against the Crone's eyes.

It was over in a minute. Cara knew the Crone had read her in just a few moments. She could have nothing left to fear, and there was nothing left to hide.

No words were spoken. The Crone turned to a shelf on the wall and picked out a bottle from amongst hundreds of others. She walked over to Cara and opened her palm with a rough motion of her hand and placed the bottle in it. She looked up into Cara's eyes and smiled. It was an odd smile. It did not communicate kindness or care. Her look was that of a victor's after a harsh battle. He might have won by cheating and was pleased with his cunning. There was a taint of condescending to it. A taste of arrogance. "Tsewang would be a bad winner and an impossible loser", Cara thought.

And yet, in spite of her unkind look, the Crone shifted something in Cara. She had such a wise, knowing, lived air about her, Cara was awed and she felt fear and respect towards this old woman. She realised suddenly that she was bowing to the Crone. She felt her heart melt and all the protection around it too. If at that moment a choice had been necessary between her own life and that of Tsewang's, she would have gladly, without hesitation offered her own up. She felt a deep sense of love and gratitude for the woman. She could not understand why. She did not like her. She wanted to get away from her. She did not want to know her or learn from her. And yet there they were, the rising feelings of admiration, respect and the warmth of those feelings held back by the cold edge of fear.

The Crone let go of Cara's hand. She placed Cara's own palm on her abdomen. Cara understood at that moment the message Tsewang was giving her. She was pregnant. Cara realised that the Crone had known from the first instant she had walked in and this was the way she chose to let her know. As soon as the flash of understanding had crossed Cara's face, the Crone let go of her hand, turned her back on Cara and walked back to the shelves where she had been when Cara first walked in.

Cara felt happy. It was the best news she could have been given and she felt as if she'd been waiting for this all her life. She walked out, her right hand still clutching the bottle and her left palm gently holding her abdomen.

She felt anxious too. How would he take the news? How do they treat expecting mothers? What do they do to them and their babies? And even more perplexing, what do they do with girls? She had not seen a single girl since she had been there. Only the slaves, women like her, there for a year and then returned back to their villages. The riders did not believe it was worth keeping a woman beyond a year. She imagined they would keep them for even less if they thought it worthwhile returning to villages more often than once a year. They left the used and picked up new, young ones instead. But what about baby girls?

Little boys ran around, got taught and trained and eventually rode out with the riders, but she had seen no little girls in the settlement, not one. What happened to them?

She pushed these disturbing thoughts away from her mind. She could not, would not, think about such things at that moment. She did not want to darken her happy mood with questions she had no answers for and doubts and fears that as yet had no foundation. Anyway, it could be a boy. She forced away any other possibilities and all questions and doubts from her mind and busied herself in the tent. How she had grown to love their tent. It was home to her, she felt comfortable and safe inside. His smell lingered in there even when he had been away for a while. It was full of happy memories for her, times of love and warmth.

She worked for the next few hours cleaning, organising, preparing food and cooking. Then she sat down to mend socks, always an endless pile of socks to mend. Sometimes she managed to get through the pile and could work on something new, a garment for her man or a throw for the bed. But mostly she mended socks.

The thought occurred to her that she had avoided Tenzin that day. She had not, as would have been her custom, ran straight to her to share her news. She stopped to ponder the reason for a moment. But she knew the answer without having to search for it long. Tenzin liked her, loved her even. If pregnancy was bad news for her, if her future would now be dubious or hard, Tenzin would not be able to hide it from her eyes, or her initial reaction. Cara was afraid of knowing the truth. She wanted to cherish the news as a purely joyful one for as long as she could. She did not want doubt or fear creeping in too soon. She would find out eventually anyway. She was not aware of how much doubt and how many dark thoughts were already lurking in the background of her mind. She focused on the positive and on her own happiness, forcing it into the forefront, willing it to outshine all else.

When he walked in later that night she was ready. She knew her face was glowing, with health, with joy, with love. She looked at him with sparkling eyes. She was shining with happiness and he smiled.

She walked up to him and as the Crone had done, but much more gently, she placed his palm on her belly. He looked down at her hand holding his there for a moment and then lifted his eyes to hers. His eyes were sparkling, but his smile had gone. His face seemed to have darkened. He walked out abruptly.

Cara felt confused. His response felt like he had slapped her in her face, or taken a whip to her chest, straight to her heart. She felt alone suddenly, isolated, sad. It was too late to go to Tenzin now. Women stayed in their tents once the riders returned. They were meant to wait for their men, making sure everything was ready for them when they came in. And when they did, they served them. The riders came first, attending to their wishes and needs were the women's priority, fulfilling their needs and wishes the sole reason the women were there. Cara didn't mind. She served her rider out of love, willingly.

She knew she was lucky. Had he been someone else, had she not loved him so deeply, she could not have done it. She would have rebelled or run away. She would have wilted and died. But she did love him and serving him made her happy.

He did not return until much later that evening. The hours of waiting had crawled past so slowly, she thought she would explode. She started to fear he would not return at all. She half expected someone else to come and fetch her, drag her out of her tent and take her somewhere to be punished, shunned, cast out, maybe killed. At any rate she would be forced away from her love.

She was lying awake in bed, anxious, worried, hurt and fearful when he walked in. He lay down behind her and placed his arm over and around her, drawing her close into himself. Nothing else. He simply held her there. And that was all she needed, all she could have ever wished for. Her whole life's happiness was contained in that one small, simple gesture. Her heart melted, her body calmed down and she fell into a peaceful, contented sleep.

He was gone when she woke up. She felt the warmth of the sun coming through the thick canvas of the tent. Normally he woke her up if she did not rise naturally, so that she could prepare breakfast while he went to wash. They then ate together before he left for the day. This morning he had left without a sound, without food, without disturbing her at all. She puzzled over his actions. He had been so gentle with her, so loving the night before. Had he left quietly so she could rest?

She also remembered his initial reaction though and that cast a dark shadow over all else no matter how vigorously she tried to push it away. Was last night his way of saying goodbye? Had he left because her news had angered him? Would she be told to pack and leave today? Would he take another woman, one that was not burdened as she was? What would become of her? Where did the riders keep pregnant women? There was so much she did not know. So much she could not understand.

So much she felt afraid of. Fear absorbed her thoughts and took control of her body. She hadn't feared the riders before they took her, or even when they did. She had not feared their anger or punishment. She had not feared speaking her mind, standing up for herself. But now she felt weak. There was another life dependent on her, that she was responsible for and had to consider. Everything seemed to matter more now. There was too much to lose. Not just her child, but having experienced it, the loss of his love would be unbearable. She felt she would die if he withdrew from her. Even the thought was painful. She could not think about it.

She tried to clear her mind of negative thoughts. She felt his love for her, his gentle protectiveness over her, the presence of which she felt even when he was away. He hid his feelings well from people, he was not open. He offered only his harsh outer surface to the world, his stern face communicated no softness, no depth of emotion. But Cara knew him too well. She saw so much more than the face he wore for the rest of the world to see. He inadvertently shared all that was inside him with her through his eyes. Those eyes that were constantly changing, at times dancing and sparkling, at other times dark and brooding. He never spoke of love, or uttered kind words, but she felt his love in the way he held her, in the way his eyes sparkled when he looked at her. And his lips smiled when she spoke. She felt there lay a warm heart beneath all that armour he shielded himself with. But had she really reached his heart? Was it even possible to deeply touch his heart? His conditioning might have made that impossible.

Were men not fickle? Would he not leave if she ceased to please him? And anyway, the laws of the riders were rigid. He would not act against them. If the law said she was now to be taken elsewhere, he would obey. He had loved her once, could she hold on to her place in his heart, or was losing it inevitable? Would centuries of rules and natural ways she did not understand guide his actions? And if so, what were these rules? What did the nature of mankind demand? How would they affect her?

After a few days her darker thoughts and concerns started to subside. His actions gradually brought calm to her heart and mind that had been in such turmoil. Her fears seemed unfounded. Nothing much seemed to change. He no longer woke her up in the mornings, but she realised that it was so that she could rest. So after the second time he crept out quietly, she resolved to hear him stir and get up with him anyway. And she did. They resumed their morning ritual. He was very gentle with her when making love and they did so less frequently now, but he didn't take another woman, or stay away for any longer than he had done previously. If anything, he became even more loving and protective over her. Her worries subsided, or at least got pushed back to some deep recess of her mind. As long as things were good, she did not want to know of any painful truths or hear of any darkness that might be hovering around her near future, preparing to take over her and her unborn.

She also resumed her visits to Tenzin. She never mentioned anything about her pregnancy to her. She guessed Tenzin knew anyway. If she did, she chose to respect Cara's silence.

Over time her worries grew fainter and life felt good once more. Time heals all and everyday life, duties, joys and work took over, so that worries, fears and concerns drew back into some distant, dark cave, hidden at the back of her mind, staying there calm and quiet.

Tenzin came when her son was born. He was a beautiful baby boy, so tiny, she could not believe his fragility. He had sparkling blue eyes, which looked up at her, large and awed. He had such incredibly soft skin. He looked so small and fragile and helpless. He demanded protection and love just by his sheer existence. He was noisy and naughty from the start though. Cara could tell he would have no problem getting his own way when he grew older. He had a natural air of confidence about him. A sense that he knew his rightful place on the planet, his right to be where he was and have what he wanted.

When her love came in after the birth, it was with large striding steps. He lifted their son above his head and looked into the eyes of his beautiful boy, with joy and love. His joy compounded hers. She could not imagine greater happiness. She felt this moment had to be the peak of her life, no joy could ever be as full and strong as what she felt at that moment. As soon as that thought occurred to her, a split second's fear crept in, fear of losing that feeling, of never feeling it again, but very quickly her happiness took over and she spent the day in a state of pure blissful whole hearted contentment and ecstatic energy.

The end of the year

It was coming up to a year. She knew the end was drawing near. Everyone knew it was. All the women shared signs of anxiety, although each manifested their tensions in their own different ways. Most of the women looked forward to their return, impatient to get back home, desperate for familiar surroundings and people, missing the proximity of loved ones around them. Yet even the most keen were dreading their return at the same time. They were afraid of how they might be treated, how people's attitudes towards them would have changed and how their feelings towards what was once so familiar and what used to be their whole world might now be different. They dreaded that some might treat them especially gently, like a fragile plant, that they might be cautious, not asking anything directly, careful not to hurt their feelings or trigger pain, yet their eyes would be scrutinising them, searching for information they dared not directly ask for. Their stares would hold quests, and although compassionate, they would be full of pity. Some were dreading their return too much to allow for any feeling of hope or any real joy. The shame they had taken on felt too heavy and they would have preferred to have been buried with that burning shame, rather than to have to face the people that had known them in a different light.

You could tell which villages were kind, protective and loving and which were harsh like Cara's. Those who came from Cara's village knew they had nothing to look forward to. They would be met with down cast eyes, stone wall faces, a life of hard work, silence and frozen feelings. Some of the others though, Cara could see by their excitement, did have something to look forward to. They walked as though although they had been used, their families would still welcome them and take them back into their bosoms. Cara wondered if even their men accepted them as they were and if they might yet still have a chance at love, marriage and children. In her village the women who returned were not offered that much compassion. They were seen as too damaged, body and soul, for any man to want to build a home with them. They were left with their families, they grew old tending to their parents, then their siblings and their siblings' children if they had any. They lived out their lives in relative loneliness in the kind of isolation that extreme experiences bring on those who survive them. The irony was that it need not be so. So many women in her village lived through that year in exile. They could have easily sought companionship in each other. But the strict, unwritten rules of the village forbade any discussion of the riders, or of the time spent with them. They were forced by their community to suffer alone in silence and to wear the mark, scorched onto their foreheads forever more. The mark that branded them broken.

Cara wondered how it was in other villages. Did the women support each other? Were the riders openly talked about, stories and experiences shared? She did not know. She did know, however, that she had been extremely lucky that year. She had seen all around her extremely abusive relationships. She had heard and seen riders treat the women terribly, with brutality, unkindness and force. Some women walked around with bruises and cuts. Three of the women brought there at the beginning of the year had died. She knew they were mostly raped. They learned submission in silence. Cara in contrast had loved her rider, his touch, their time together. She had taken on the role of a willing, happy wife, not of a slave. She could not imagine what their tormented hearts carried, and what she caught glimpses of was dark and unbearable. She was grateful for her luck, but then separation was going to be so much harder for her. Some women had died inwardly during their year here. Cara would die the day she left.

Cara's thoughts went back to her village. Although it was the women who were taken by the riders that were branded as damaged, she felt that it was those who remained behind that were more truly damaged. They were the ones who were unable to accept the course of nature, of men, unable to accept the return of those they had once loved. Why were her kin men and women so harsh, so cold in their hearts? Had their lives been harder than all these other people's? And if it had, was that a sufficient excuse? How could those who never even experienced what she and the other women had be so judgemental, their actions shrouded in a protective cloak of ignorance. What pleasure or satisfaction did they get out of shunning these women? How did holding them separate from themselves make them feel better, cleaner, higher?

Cara dreaded her mother the most. A year apart had worn down the compassion she used to feel towards her mother. She resented her mother for not being able to love her. Why had she withheld love from her own daughter all her life? Cara had received love from her rider and from Tenzin. Why then could her own mother not have shown her even the slightest fragment of such warmth? Why had she not been capable of finding any feeling in her heart for her own child?

Cara pushed thoughts of her mother away from her mind. That day would come, far too soon, when she would have to face her again, hear her voice, obey her orders. Her pride rose up in anger, her soul rebelled. She held those down too.

Only Cara out of all the women who had been brought there, was dreading leaving, because she did not want to leave at all, because departure would mean a greater misery than she had ever known before. Only Cara wanted to stay. And she wanted to stay with her whole heart and soul. She would have given up anything else for the chance of remaining where she was, the one place she had experienced the feelings of belonging, being at home, of love, being appreciated and living with joy.

Most of the women felt that their one year sentence, the slavery brought on to too many young women, transforming them from mere girls in to bitter, hardened women, was nearing completion at last and they were glad. They would be able go back to their villages, comfortable in the knowledge that no matter how many times they saw the riders ride into their town from that day onwards, no matter how many times they heard the call dreaded by everyone who had heard it once, "they're coming", they would never feel afraid for themselves or anxious about their futures again. They would not be taken a second time. It would be over, done, in the past. The dreaded experience never to be repeated or expected and feared again. No unknown shadow would linger waiting for them in an uncertain future. What was passed was passed. The rest of their lives would be completed along known, well trodden paths. That knowledge brought a sense of calm and peace with it. But Cara's feelings were different. The unknown attracted and excited her. She desired adventure. She wanted to see more, learn more and grow wise, mature and old. She loved surprises. For her the unknown was not a heavy dark cloud hiding the sun, it was an adventure park, a forest covered in light mist, so that each ride or each step brought some new experiences and each experience till then unknown joys.

Cara felt alone and isolated in her feelings. She did not want to leave. She was happy where she was. But there was not a soul she could share her feelings with. They would not understand her. In fact they would judge and resent her. People tend to have a fear of those who are different and are not afraid of being themselves and standing their own ground. They like to push them out to the fringes of society, hoping to keep themselves and their own narrow ways of living safe. Cara was too wild for them anyway, too head strong, too independent, too lively, too happy.

She felt a shudder pass through her body as she wondered what would become of her son. Leaving her rider, her love, brought agonising pain to her heart, she dared not linger with that thought. But the thought of losing her son brought panic. The sensation was too strong and although she tried to, she could not push the fear away.

She heard the commotion early one morning. They were gathering up the women they had brought a year ago. Every single one of them was being led into the centre clearing. She held her boy, willing him to be still and quiet. Receiving comfort from his warmth against her skin and his fresh, clean smell close to her nostrils. She tried in vain to calm her own galloping heart by holding her son close to her chest. Maybe they would forget her. She heard the footsteps, the shouted orders, the ruffling of skirts as the women were hurried by. She heard them gathering in the open space at the centre of the camp. She heard and felt their anxiety, she could taste it. Her son started to cry. She tried to settle him. "Quiet, they'll hear you". She was hoping they'd forget her, knowing they never forgot anything. And even if she were forgotten, she could not hide forever. What would happen when they found her out? What kind of punishment would be hers? But those worries were for later, not now. All that mattered now, all she felt aware of was the need to stay, one more moment, one more day, for as long as she could.

The commotion lasted for what seemed an eternity. She could feel her whole body shaking violently. She had lost control over her limbs. Every passing second her anxiety increased. Her mind was in turmoil. Her heart ached from over exertion. Her breath was shallow, fast and ineffective. And yet minute after minute passed and no one came. She heard more commotion, even louder than before, and then the sounds gradually growing quieter as they moved away from her, until she could hear nothing more. She started shaking too violently to hold her baby anymore. He was crying desperately now, screaming at the top of his voice, but she placed him on the bed and collapsed to the floor at his feet. She held her knees close to her chest, her arms wrapped around them and started rocking to and fro, shaking violently and crying.

He did not return for weeks. None of them did. The camp was quiet except for a few elderly men and some young children, the older boys had ridden out with them. There weren't that many of either, only the useful were kept on, and only for as long as they remained useful.

She had no idea why she had been left behind or what it meant. She found it impossible to do anything that day. She stayed in their tent, not daring to venture out. She could not work, or sit still for long, her mind was in turmoil and her heart was racing. She lay down many times during the day, when all energy and life left her and she could no longer sit or stand. The rest of the time she rocked her son, or walked up and down the small tent with him in her arms. She felt afraid, anxious, fatigued.

As night drew in, she felt she had to leave her tent and venture outside. She wanted to know what had happened. She had to find out how they would react to her still being there. She could not put the suspense off for any longer. Bad news was better than no news.

It was a windy, cool evening. The sky held too many clouds for any stars to shine through. There was a smell of unrest in the air. Even the animals were restless, a cacophony of sounds rising from them, shouts and cries coming from all directions.

In spite of the commotion outside and the restlessness gathered like heavy clouds in the air, the camp remained quiet. Most of those who had remained had retired to their tents. The odd person she did come across looked at her as they always had, said as little or as much as they always did. Cara was first confused, but gradually she grew calmer. It seemed to her that everyone knew she was still there and it was okay. Even though she still did not understand why and she still had no idea what was to eventually become of her, the normalcy of their treatment helped her subdue her fears. She was able to sleep that night.

For the next few days she worked hard as always. She worked and ate with the others and took care of her boy. She still felt confused when she thought about the meaning of her being allowed to stay. No one had explained anything to her.

No one had dropped the smallest hint or clue and she had not dared ask anything. She did not want them to know she was afraid it might have been an oversight. Perhaps they had not been told she would stay, but they thought it had been planned, because she was still there. Perhaps the truth was she had simply been forgotten and if she asked questions, they would realise the truth and know she no longer belonged with them. She could not take that risk. She told herself she had to be calm and confident. If she acted calm they would think that her staying on with them had been a conscious decision. Yet she still feared something would change, she feared they might throw her out once they realised she shouldn't be there. She kept telling herself it was okay, they didn't make such mistakes and that she belonged there, but the fear ran underneath even her most confident moments.

Days and weeks... No one told her anything. No one's treatment of her changed. Yet the silence surrounding her was suffocating. The silence that returned as an answer to all her unasked questions. The silence in her head and heart, waiting to be filled, dreading to be filled. Hoping, waiting, dreading...

Her big moment of truth would be when her rider returned. She would find out everything then. She wanted that moment to come, was anxious for it, impatient. And yet, at the same time, she dreaded that moment, feared it. She both wanted to delay it forever and fast forward it to the very moment she was in.

Her emotions plummeted from one extreme to another and she could find no moment of true inner calm. Fear and hope alternated within her. Sometimes they joined hands and pressed against her together. She hid in her fear, unable to qualm it. Her hope carried too many doubts with it to stand alone with strength.

He returned with the rest of them a couple of months later. His time away had passed too slowly for her, every day taking as long as a lifetime. She had spent most of that time feeling afraid, tiny and alone in a hostile world. Sometimes she found herself lying in bed at night, unable to sleep, unable to cry or scream, with a large, heavy, dark weight crushing down on her chest, preventing her from breathing. The dark weight of the unknown incapacitating her. The unknown brought with it fear, surrounding her like clouds during the day and pressing down on her in the dead quiet of the night, when it was at its most overwhelming, when she could not find release and distraction in chores and activities.

Sometimes she felt the walls caving in on her, moving in closer and closer. She could see they were physically at the same distance they had always been, but even as she stared at them, aware of their stillness, she could still feel them pressing on her skin, through her flesh, on her bones, crushing her, rendering her immobile. She wanted to cry, but no sound ever left her body. Her movements became constrained, her sight limited, a kind of fog hovering over her eyes, separating her being from life and the world surrounding her. She no longer noticed the changing sky, the trees and flowers. She could not taste what she ate. Sometimes she wasn't able to eat at all.

She wanted to die at times to save herself from potential pain, but then she'd feel hope and she knew that if all ended well, it would have been worth every second of uncertainty and fear she had experienced. It would be okay once he returned. She was torn between fear of heartbreak and wanting to avoid it even at the price of death, and hope. She experienced moments of elation when she held her baby boy and a voice within her reassured her, telling her she was still there, it was okay.

The morning she heard the riders approach, she was holding her baby, staring sightless into the distance. The noise jerked her into startled awareness. Her breath stopped. She waited,both with excitement and impatience and a cold fear, as if expecting her impending doom.

The riders were in the main court. There was much moving around, hustle and bustle, shouts, laughter. She didn't see him for hours. Only once it started to quieten down did she feel his approach. He walked over to her in his usual striding, vigorous steps. She could tell straight away that he had known she would be there. So it had not been an oversight. She waited, silent, immobile. He pulled their baby out of her arms and twirled him around above his head, lowered him to his face and kissed him on his nose. Then he lowered him back into her arms, placed his arm around her shoulders, turned her around and gently pushed her back into their home.

Her son was an absolute delight to her. She had less time to study with Tenzin since her son's birth, but it was a sacrifice she was willing to make. He was a happy boy, smiling, chuckling, playing with his tiny fingers and toes up in the air all the time. She loved him dearly. He looked like her rider already and that made her love him even more.

She spent most of her time taking care of him, feeding him, playing with him, holding him. Her hours were defined by his schedule. When she slept, when she was awake, when she could work, what she could and could not do with her time, all depended on this tiny little being. He governed her life and she loved that power he held over her. She found it funny that this tiny, fragile little creature could control her every feeling and action so completely. That it could be the source of such infinite love.

Her rider loved their boy too. As soon as he walked in each evening, he would look around for his son. If he was awake he would hold him in his hands and raise him up to the skies, twirling him around, pinching his chubby arms and legs, kissing him and speaking to him. If their son was asleep, he would gaze at him with fond eyes and utter an inward prayer for him. He was considerate of them both, minding their moods, taking care of their needs and providing for their comfort and ease. She never found herself in need of anything any more, he noticed and took care of everything he could before she had even noticed the need. He had also started to bring them little treats from time to time. Cara, as unused to luxury and treats as she was, loved that special care and attention and enjoyed any treat with the delight and excitement of a child. She felt a little embarrassed at first, imagining herself as ridiculous, but she saw that her love enjoyed watching her as much as she enjoyed his gift, so she allowed her excitement to overflow, without worrying about keeping her joy under control.

Cara was happy. She had never really experienced life with a warm, loving family. Now she had the most incredible home and family she could have ever dreamed of and she felt grateful. She could not believe her luck. She realised just how much she had missed out on as a child.

Her life had changed beyond recognition and the change was sublime. She belonged, she was loved and cherished, her wishes respected. She was protected and cared for. And their boy was a treasure to behold. She could not understand why her mother would have chosen to kill the potential for such joy and love in her own life. Why would she have held back such a wonderful experience not only from her children, but from herself as well? Loving was just as wonderful as being loved and Cara could not understand why a person would choose a life that allowed no space for either. How could she have denied herself and her family such natural feelings? And to what end? She had gained nothing from her cold, unloving treatment of them other than a growing sense of unhappiness and bitterness within herself, which in turn had fed her resentment towards her children as if her unhappiness was all their fault. An unending cycle of destruction and harm, inwards and outwards.

Sometimes Cara wondered if her mother would feel grief and a sense of loss herself if she could see what she had missed out on and what she could have created and how happy they might have all been. But in her heart Cara understood that her mother was not like her, that she was incapable of this kind of love, or joy, or pleasure. For her mother everything was a duty, duty was a burden, and burdens were to be despised.

Cara wanted to talk to Tenzin about her mother. She wanted to understand her mother so that she could forgive her fully. She wanted to learn what had blocked her mother's heart so, what had turned it to stone and if there was any way of thawing it. But she could never find the words to voice her questions. There was always so much else to discuss, and there was a resistance in Cara against the topic. Maybe she was afraid of what Tenzin would say. She left these questions unasked day after day.

After her baby was born, Tenzin brought her some herbs and told her to boil them in water and drink a cup every day. Cara asked what they were for. She said simply "no more babies". Cara was taken aback. She thought she might have misunderstood. She asked Tenzin what she meant, but the only reply she received was "you have been lucky child, you won't be next time. No more babies. Babies bring no good to a woman in this place".

Cara did not answer. She did not ask why babies were bad for a woman and what Tenzin meant with her being lucky this once, and not next time. She felt herself turn cold inside. That horrible shiver she had experienced months ago ran through her again. She felt afraid for a moment. Then shrugged the shiver and the fear off. She was here. She was well. Her boy was with her. Her rider had kept her. There was no point digging up negative possibilities and omens, bringing in doom and gloom to her bright, happy life.

She knew well it was an exception that she had been kept

on after a year. She had no idea why they had chosen to. She did not know for how long she would be allowed to stay. Or what might be expected of her in return. All she knew was that she would do as Tenzin said. One day she would find out the answers to all her questions. At this moment, this one time in her life, she wasn't interested in answers, she was interested in her happiness. "Sometimes oblivion is bliss", she thought.

Tenzin's words brought back the oddness of the situation to her though, and left a shadow in her heart, a dull weight in her chest. Surface thoughts she could throw away, but this deeper shadow was not so easy to shake off. She had been so busy since the turn of that year and so happy that she had managed very successfully to keep fears and doubts away, but suddenly they returned with a sense of urgency. The tone of Tenzin's voice had brought this feeling up from within her. There was an underlying threat and concern in her tone and the truth of the threat was that it was non-negotiable. Cara started to think about what had happened and what had been said, searching for a clue. Why would they have kept her on? Many women had children. They had all been returned. In fact there were no other women who had been there longer than a year, except for the three crones, and they were old, wise women, with their unique skills and valuable place in this small society. The riders needed them.

But then maybe that was it. Dare she hope? Tenzin was getting old and Cara was her disciple. She had already learned a lot. Tenzin was pleased with Cara's progress. She had said many times that Cara was a fast learner. Maybe they were letting her stay to learn Tenzin's trade, so that she could take over when the time came.

Cara liked the idea. She wanted to be as wise as her and to read the stars as well as she did, guiding and helping people with her knowledge. She wanted to be of service to the community in that way. And most of all, she wanted an excuse to stay on.

As attractive as that idea was, there was yet another

possibility that her heart wished for even more. She would have loved to believe that her rider had made her stay possible, because he would not, could not let her go. She wished that he had demanded she stay, that he loved her enough to take a stance against the rules of the riders, that he reciprocated her feelings for him with a strong, lasting, deep love like hers. But she dared not think that. Nobody broke the rules and she could not believe he would have either. She didn't want to let her hopes rise too high. She feared she was wrong and the disappointment would have been too much for her. But in spite of what she told herself and how hard she steered away from the thought, the wish was there in a corner of her soul nonetheless. Hidden, mostly even from her own view, but there.

Whatever the reason, she was grateful to God and the riders she was still there. She had always been a zestful, hard worker, and now she strived even harder. She had a kind word to say to everyone she saw and she resolved in her heart that she would try especially hard with those she didn't like. She belonged to all those who belonged here and she must serve them all the same. She promised herself she would study even more attentively and diligently with Tenzin, although she found it hard to keep that promise with a baby depending on her at all times. There was simply not enough time for everything. She did her best though.

She named her son Joseph, in memory of her lost brother. Her love did not argue against the name she chose. He accepted the name without question, as if it was natural for her to decide.

During one of their rounds, Tenzin and Cara went to see a woman who, they had been told, would no longer eat or leave her bed. After checking her health, Tenzin left the tent and Cara found herself alone with a young woman she had hardly ever seen around. She could see the woman had been crying, but apart from that and looking rather tired and thin, she did not seem to have anything wrong with her.

The woman turned to her suddenly and cried "how do you do it?"

Cara felt amazed at this sudden outburst of emotion and her hard voice demanding an explanation to she knew not what. She could not at first understand what the woman was referring to. The woman did not seem to notice the puzzled expression on Cara's face. She started to cry, turning her back to Cara.

Cara waited for her tears to lose some of their violent energy and then asked her gently "how do I do what?"

"How can you live here? How can you bare being treated like this? How can you want to go on? How can you smile? How can you not want to kill yourself?"

Cara felt a desire to tell this woman of her happiness, to lecture her about changing her perspective. She wanted to somehow force this woman into finding joy and light in her duties and comfort in her surroundings. But something stopped her. She was wary of judging this poor woman and diminishing her experience. Instead she decided to find out more. Maybe if she understood the woman, she would better be able to help her.

"Why do you want to kill yourself? Surely, no matter how bad your experience here, you know it will be over soon. Then you can return your village and live your life as you would like to, as you used to"

"How could I? I cannot. The girl that left her village months ago is dead. She no longer exists. I have nothing in common with her except for my name. I would be returning a dead person, an anguished soul. My soul has already given up on life. Why drag my body around this earth for any longer? What would be the point?"

"You might find life and joy again. Time heals everything. These days will seem very far away to you once you have left here"

"I might move far away from this place, but this place will never leave me, no matter how far I travel and for how long I am gone. My experience is a part of me and this place has been etched into my skin, my very being. It will never leave me"

Cara did not understand such hopelessness and desperation, but she wanted to. Her heart ached for the woman and she wanted to ease her pain, if at all possible.

"Tell me about it" she said, not able to find any specific questions to ask her, "tell me of your experience here. Tell me what it is that has etched its way into your very soul and killed it, as you put it"

The woman started sobbing once more and at first speech and clear words were not possible. But eventually, with the help of Cara's presence, the woman started to calm down. She turned to face Cara and said "I will".

Cara listened to the woman's story for a long time. The woman told it well. She spoke from her heart. She had fully experienced her pain and was able to describe it and all that had created it. Cara listened to her as she spoke of daily abuse, physical, mental, sexual. Of living in fear day after day, until even that fear had died and a numb emptiness had taken its place. She told of her desire to cleanse herself and feel that she could not, ever, be clean again, no matter how hard she tried. She told her of nights of anger, overcome by fear, in turn overcome by desperation. She told of darkness, not being able to see, not being able to breathe.

"I have given up you see" she said finally. "I ask for nothing, want nothing except that I be left alone to die in my own way. I want to feel all that is raging within me, every little bit of it, until there is nothing left and the fire dies out naturally. I want all that suffering and horror to play itself out in my memories, my mind and emotions and my body, so that I can leave this world without taking any of it with me. So that all that poison dies with my body on this earth. I want to let them rage and take over, but gradually they will wear themselves out, as a physical body does and they will leave me in peace. That is all I expect of my life now. Let me be. Please"

Cara nodded and got up slowly. She kissed the woman's forehead and left the tent quietly. Tenzin was waiting for her outside. She walked over to her and took her hand, patting it gently. Then she led her away from the scene of such pain. Yet there Cara had also witnessed so much strength and courage.

The woman's image stayed with Cara for days. She could hear her voice and her final plea in her mind. Thinking of the woman brought her discomfort. Yet at the same time she felt herself fill with hope too. Hope that there was strength and understanding in the world. Hope that people could find the right way, each way unique to each person, each one different, each needing courage and will and yet everyone of them possible if one tried. There had been a determination in the woman that Cara had not seen in anyone else before. An inner strength that would not be broken.

In spite of the awe Cara felt for the woman, she did not feel comfortable thinking about her. She did not want to see the evil side of the settlement. She did not like to hear any ill spoken of the riders and their ways. She did not want even the hint of a cloud to pass over her clear blue sky. She knew hers was not the whole story, but she did not care. She preferred to love them and not see their faults. She did not want any stories of pain and abuse to tarnish her love for her life there. So she put the woman away from her mind and eventually forgot about her story.

Everything has an ending

It had been seven years since she had left her birth place and natural family. In her own village she had never felt at home the way she felt in this little settlement of riders, nothing more than a well organised camp site inhabited by roving rangers. She had never felt she really belonged amongst her own kin folk, yet here she belonged. She had a role in the community, she could help and serve and in return she received gratitude and a feeling of worth born out of usefulness. She felt loved, she had a family and someone to share her life with.

Even though she had always been a hard worker and a kind, gentle soul, she had never been greeted with warmth or gratitude amongst her village people. Nothing she had done there was ever worth thanking her or smiling at her for. No role she played had been deemed significant or useful. No one had cared about her. She had not felt loved or wanted. She had been an outsider, a misfit.

Here she felt she truly belonged. She found ease of being here in the wilderness, amongst the riders. She made friends amongst them and always greeted them with warmth wherever she went. Each year new women were brought. She had learned to accept the transitory nature of their existence there and to feel compassion for their confusion and struggles. She made friends with some, got close to a few. Then as the end of the year approached she withdrew, knowing they would all leave soon. She offered her smile, her support and advice when it was needed. She comforted the sad, listened to those with heavy hearts, answered questions, offered guidance and help.

All those years, there had still been no other exceptions. No one apart from her had stayed on beyond their year. She had not been pregnant again and her love never asked her why not. He seemed happy with the way things were and he was kind and attentive to both her and their son. Unless he was away, he always came back in the evenings to play with Jo and to spend time with her. She thought he was happy with his home, with her, with his family.

Her love for him had grown stronger with passing years, although she could hardly have believed it possible for her to love him any more than she already had at the end of their first year together. To her he was like her own flesh and blood. She would have given her life to save his. Any injury he had, she wished she could bear his pain instead of him. His smile gave her joy, his happiness pleasure. His presence gave her an essence of life, richer and more essential to her than oxygen or water.

Every year, as the time neared for the women to be taken away and returned to their 'home's, she had a stirring of anxiety, as if she caught it in the wind. What if this time they took her? What if his love for her had grown old? What if he was tired of her? What if she hadn't proved her worth? She always pushed the thoughts away. She was safe at that moment and she could not bear to think beyond that.

The time of leaving had drawn near and passed each year, with her still in the settlement, the decision made to her benefit one more time. And each time she felt a renewal of gratitude, all be it slightly shadowed with doubts and "but why?"s.

She had been allowed to stay year after year, yet those stirrings of anxiety always returned. They grew less intense with time, less panicky, but there in the background nonetheless. No one had ever told her why she had been kept on, and without understanding the reason she could not feel completely safe. But she had not been taken away and that was all that really mattered. The day of leaving came and went and she remained, relieved each time. And tired, worn out from the uncertainty and fear she slept long hours once they had left.

The time for departure was nearing again. There was the

usual subdued background noise of preparations, anxieties and anticipations of the women. She had withdrawn for the past week, she did not take part in any of the preparations, leave takings or camaraderie. She never did. She belonged with the riders, not with the women and she did not like saying goodbye. Their excitement and tension felt too heavy for her and she tried to distance herself from it all.

Jo was playing with stones he had gathered. He was a lively boy, running around, causing havoc whenever he could. She smiled as she watched him. The sight of her son calmed her.

Then she saw them. Two riders walking up to her. Not her man, not her love, but two others, two that were his friends. They were walking straight towards her. Her heart stopped. They did not meet her questioning eyes, they looked straight ahead and picked up a satchel lying at the far end of the tent. They started placing items in it. They were gathering her few belongings.

Then she saw Tenzin standing at the entrance to her tent. She hadn't heard her approach. She had no idea how long she had been standing there. She felt a myriad of feelings overwhelm her all at once, all those strangled feelings that had been frozen in her with the approach of the two men. Fear, despair, prayers, hope, anger. She ran over to Tenzin and let out a short sharp cry of anguish. She collapsed at Tenzin's feet, unable to hold back her tears. Tenzin walked past her to her son and gently took hold of his little hand. Then she returned back to Cara, took her hand also and led them out to the gathering place.

Fear, shock and pain numbed her. She followed quietly and stood still where she was left. She saw and heard nothing of what was going on around her. Her body felt cold, too cold to ever thaw again, her eyes glazed over.

She could feel his presence, but dared not look up, not just yet. He was letting her go, she understood that much. He was done with her. Why had he kept her on for so long if he was going to chuck her out eventually anyway? Every passing year making the inevitable departure and separation harder and harder for her, her love growing, her place in the settlement becoming more comfortable, her mind more certain of her belonging there amongst them. Her heart and worries easing over time into security. It would have been a little easier after the first year compared to after seven beautiful years with him. She had expected it then. But now? Why now? She had grown to believe he loved her as she loved him, as deeply. She had grown to believe that he looked forward to returning to her, lying in her arms, that her smile warmed him inside just as much as his smile warmed her. What had happened? Had she done something wrong? Or was he simply tired of her? Bored, fed up, done. Ready for fresh smells, fresh bodies.

She had never understood why he had kept her on. She could not understand how come he was able to when none of the others did or could. But this was worse. If he could keep her on, why was he now letting her go? Throwing her away, done with her at last as all the other women had been cast away year after year.

It hurt too deeply. She felt she could not survive the pain. Her heart was being seared, torn, cut up. The pain was so deep and whole, she could not bare it. She could not stay with it any longer. She wished for death, unconsciousness, anything but being there. And yet she could not move. There was no escape. Whatever was to come would happen. She could not escape her fate. She had no say over her future. The decision had been reached without her understanding, let alone consent. She felt trapped.

The rest of the journey was a blur for her. She ate, drank, slept, walked, fed her son, did all that was expected of her without a sound. She obeyed, never initiated. She was too numb and unconscious to be able to think or feel. She just did as she was told.

She hadn't even noticed her surroundings becoming

familiar as they approached her old village. She hadn't even noticed they had arrived when they stopped in the main square. She hadn't even noticed them lead her away from the rest of the group, holding on to her boy by his small hand, clutching it tightly. She hadn't even noticed the gathering of village folk around her, people she would have recognised if she had still eyes capable of seeing.

She felt his presence as he drew near on his horse. She felt him come right up to her as she stared blank and unseeing at the ground. She felt him pull at her son, their son, their holding hands torn apart. She felt his warm breath as it came close to her face. His rough fingers as they stroked the hair away from her forehead, his moist lips as they touched her eyelids, one after the other.

Then she felt him turn his horse around and start to move away. She felt the cold emptiness in her palm where seconds ago she had felt the warmth of her son's little hand. She felt a volcano of despair, of death and nothingness, of loss and loneliness. She felt her insides slaughtered, ripped out, sharp knives and daggers scraping along the inside walls of her body, her heart screaming with anguish.

She heard the scream as it shattered the silence, the clouds breaking apart, darkness overtaking her whole being. She didn't realise it was her own body that had released the scream. She wasn't there, not really, not any more. She just heard a shattering scream, one that would wrench anyone's soul apart.

Then nothing. Blank. Darkness. "Death has come to me, thank God" she thought. Then the hard slap of the ground against her cheek as she ended up unconscious to the world on the ground. The cold, harsh sand. Emptiness. Darkness. And so much pain. God the pain. She prayed for death, but the earth under her face was still there. She could hear sounds around her as a crowd gathered, some hesitantly prodding her, moving her. She heard the hooves of horses growing distant. She had been abandoned, left there with her despair, her broken heart, in darkness. He had given her everything and then taken it all back from her. Her son, her love, her life, all stolen, grabbed away, leaving nothing but a broken, empty shell. One she wished would crumple into the soil, leaving no body behind, setting her free.

She knew she had to leave. She felt an urgent burning need to escape. She wanted to get away from the suffocating silence, the oppressing indifference and lack of compassion she received daily from her family, the four walls that closed in on her every moment, the chores she got through, mindlessly, unconsciously.

Where could she go? She had nowhere, knew nowhere and had no one. All she knew was that she had to leave. Even the thought of leaving passed through her body like a cool, relieving breeze. But most of the time she lacked the strength or will to do anything. Although her soul welcomed the idea of leaving, her body lacked the energy to do it. She felt trapped and lost. She tried to come up with a plan, but beyond stepping out the front door, she could see no path in front of her, not a glimmer of light to show the way. All around her was darkness. She was suffocating, drowning, sinking in relentless, dark, dense quicksand.

She lay awake at night, unable to breathe, until she lost consciousness through sheer exhaustion. She wanted to die, but did not have the means or enough will to go through with that either. She wondered at her lack of anger towards God or her rider. She felt nothing most of the time. No anger, no sadness, no loss. Just a sense of all pervading muted numbness. Even her heart felt moulded over. If it were stabbed again, there would have been no sound, no pain, no sensation at all. A cushioned step on moss, soundless, without resonance, non-existent to the world. Everything around her and inside, her whole being were silence and death.

Her mother had been kind enough, as so far as she was capable of kindness. She wasn't really an affectionate, caring person and she did not care much for Cara, but she had left her alone mostly, which to Cara seemed like the greatest act of kindness possible. As long as Cara got her chores done, kept quiet and didn't complain, didn't drag her feet, or take too long and didn't cry, her mother treated her with distant silence, only a slight disdain perceptible in her treatment of her. That suited Cara. She did not want sympathy. She could not bear questions. She worked, because it was the only thing she could do, it helped the hours pass. She could not cry anyway, her heart was dry, there were no tears, no sorrow, just a numb, aching pain. Her insides were frozen lifeless and she didn't mind that too much. The cutting, searing pain she had felt when he left was too unbearable to endure ever again. She preferred this darkness and the numb, mouldy feeling of death within her to the aching heartbreak she knew was hidden beneath it all.

Her life revolved around her internal world. She had been pretty successful in fitting everyone else and their lives around it. Her dad went about his business, working wherever he could find some work, leaving at the crack of dawn and returning after she had retreated to her bed. She knew he didn't work that late. She could tell from his harsh, a little too loud, sometimes a little too merry, sometimes randomly angry and excited voice that his daily routine included after work drinks in the common house. It was called the common house, because it was like a communal hub for the men, although it was nothing more than a small shack, with dirty tables and stools. Most of the village men could be found there in the evenings. There was always a fire blazing out, bits of meat cooking, a soup and some bread nearby and most importantly lots of alcohol. Theirs was a harsh life with much struggle and pain. No one resented them their bit of camaraderie and fun. The women were never included though.

Her mother made use of her dad as best she could. Getting him to run errands and do stuff around the place when he was around, taking most of his earnings when she went to deliver his lunch, personally by hand. They all knew it was not out of kindness or thoughtfulness that she took him lunch to his work. She went because if she didn't collect the money at lunch time, he would use it all at the common house in the evening.

Her mother's daily routine was as social as her fathers. She was up later than everyone else, complaining about the cold and her creaking joints, and that she hadn't been able to sleep because of her husband's snoring. Cara wondered if her mother hated him, or just liked complaining. In truth he gave her plenty of excuses to vent her bitter suppressed anger and disappointment in life.

She would then revive the fire. If someone hadn't brought in bracken and logs for the fire all hell would break loose, that was an oversight none of the members of the family had ever repeated twice. The fire was always allowed to gradually burn out as soon as they sat down for dinner in the evening. The nights were cold, but they were used to it, sleeping in as many layers as they could.

Dinner was a miserable time of the day for Cara. Their father never turned up, their mother complained, bickered, told her and her sister, Julie, off and gave orders, reminding them in bossy tones what their duties for that night and the next morning were, complaining about things she saw as oversights, mistakes or badly done jobs. The two of them sat opposite her quietly, looking forward to the silence and solitude they would find once the day was over and they could close their eyes in the dark safety of their beds.

Once the fire was going to her satisfaction, she placed a pot of water over it for the coffee and ate her breakfast. It was Julie's job to have her bread ready for her. If they were lucky, there would be some stew or soup left over from the day before, but that was rare. Usually it was just bread. Once, to show her gratitude for the help Cara had given her in collecting wood throughout her illness, their neighbour had given them some butter. Cara got to try it once. It tasted so rich and creamy, she felt guilty eating it. It melted in her mouth and tasted of luxury,

luxury she knew she would never really know intimately and would only ever get small flittering tastes of, and even those would be rare. Her experience with buttered bread was a once only event.

Her mother, once she had eaten and drank, gave the girls orders for the day and spent the rest of the morning at one neighbour or another, gossiping, bickering and complaining. She came home for lunch, which Julie would have ready for them all. Another silent, painful family meal. Once she finished eating, her mother took over his lunch to her father and went off to a neighbour once again. The women also had drinks. They had theirs in someone's home during the afternoons. These were unpleasant, dreary gatherings, the irritating drone of the complaining, bickering women going on and on like a small swarm of flies searching for dirt and garbage and lingering a little when they found some, only to move on once again in search of fresh rubbish.

All the women had grown negative and bitter over the years, in their own slightly varying ways. They no longer had any expectations from life. They hoped or wished for nothing. They cared for nothing, except passing the time, wasting the hours and days, wishing them speed in passing. Doing their best to live out their torturous prison sentences here on earth. Mindless bickering and alcohol had a mind numbing effect and they were grateful for that at least. They resented the world they were born into and with that resentment came a hatred for everything and everyone else in it.

Cara could not stand the meal times any more. Those hours were the hardest to endure. The rest of the time she was able to find some sense of peace within herself. When working, her mind was numb, her body busy, time went by fast enough. When lying in bed in the darkness and silence of the night, although it seemed to her that the very air surrounding her was trying to suffocate her, at least she was alone in her suffering. No onlookers, no bitterness seeping in and surrounding her from her mother, just the quiet of the night and her aching heart. She could deal with that most nights. But some nights were worse, when her heart seemed to thaw a little and the excruciating pain returned. Just like when her fingers had frozen working outdoors in the winter and she came back into warmth; as her fingers came alive they woke into the world with a similar searing pain.

The pain was unbearable, yet somehow she did bear it, she always survived each day only to start again the next morning. How, she could never understand, but she remained alive. She wished with all her heart she would not, but she always did. Even in her agony there was comfort though, compared to sitting there in front of her mother, listening to her complaints, complaints that seemed so pointless and petty to Cara, so bitter and useless. In the past she had felt compassion for her mother, now she mostly felt indifference, except for the times she noticed anger and hatred surface in her before she managed to squash them back down, knowing those feelings were unacceptable.

She could feel her mother's resentment. Her mother resented her lost, but at least for a short while experienced happiness, her broken heart, her quiet acquiescence and dutiful, uncomplaining life. She felt her mother would have liked her better if she had turned to drink and complaining, if she had shouted or rebelled. Then at least her mother could have shouted back, vented her own frustration and anger. Or maybe she would have found in Cara's acted out misery a kindred spirit, one that she could understand much better than Cara's stoic bearing of it all with inner strength, in silence. Quiet, dutiful, kind as Cara was, her mother could not understand her. She could find no excuse to hate her out aloud, so her unspoken hatred and resentment grew inside her, covered, locked up, pushed down, each day feeding the poison in her heart a little more. Her eyes were full of hate when she looked at Cara. Her orders full of malice and Cara didn't have the energy to care.

Cara paid no attention to the continuous negative remarks,

subtle insults, nasty rebukes. She could feel her mother's hatred, but she would not acknowledge it consciously. She kept telling herself "poor mother, such a hard, unhappy life, she doesn't hate me, she's just tired, she would not wish me evil, she's just carried away with life's hardships, doing her best, trying to do her bit". She thought if she kept repeating such things to herself, she would eventually believe them. If nothing else, these thoughts enabled her to go on complying with her mother's wishes and demands. Otherwise who knows how she would have reacted. In her heart she felt the excuses she made for her mother didn't fit. She knew they were lies. But somehow she preferred the lies to truths. They made her family life bearable. They enabled her to keep playing her role as her mother's hated slave. Cara had enough heartbreak in her heart, enough pain already. She didn't need any more. She did need to get away though. Soon. She had to get away.

She must have dosed off. It was so hard to sleep, but tiredness eventually took over, transporting her into a more easy, unconscious darkness. She felt tired all the time since her return. She had no energy for anything, no will to do anything, no reason to keep moving or working, apart from the steady, constant automatic guidance of her body. Any sleep she got was never enough. It failed to nourish her, or to rejuvenate her weary, dying soul. It was welcome nonetheless, for the thoughtless, feelingless, unaware darkness it brought to her. In the short period of unconscious sleep no painful memories or thoughts haunted her mind, no bitterness tainted her heart.

She suddenly remembered what had woken her up. She'd had a dream. She tried to catch the dream that had already fled her consciousness. She could not remember it. At first her mind was blank. Then she remembered the dream had brought her an understanding, some kind of guidance. It had told her that she needed to give something up. But what? She had nothing left to give up. She had nothing in the world.

She puzzled over the tiny glimpse of her dream. Even as she searched her heart and mind, asking herself the question, she already knew what the answer was. "I need to give up everything. I feel I have nothing left worth giving up, nothing I care about keeping, yet I'm still clinging on to my life. I'm holding onto my family, as unwelcoming as they are. I'm staying on at this village, giving myself to their way of life, sharing their lives. I eat their food, sleep under their roof. I have my chores, a mother to obey and a sister that I love, I have my values, my past, my memories, my questions, and even though buried deep, practically unreachable, I know I still have hopes and dreams. My life here, my family, they offer me security of sorts, something to do, somewhere to live, somewhere to belong. I have an idea of who I am, what I should do, what I would like to do, how I should live, a way I define myself. And all of this needs to go. I need to let go of it all. I need to leave everything behind. I need to die completely if I want to live. I need to die to break free, to get away from all that binds me to the darkness, all the mould that's growing over my soul every minute of every day. I need to feel death, so that I can feel alive once more, to hear the screaming last cry of the dying, so that I can wake up in peace. I must die to this world, die to myself as I know myself. I need to learn to let go. Otherwise I will grow colder and number. I will sink deeper into dark mud, my eyes will glaze over further leaving no sight but blank fog. And I will live the life of a bitter, tired, unhappy ghost forever"

She felt strength and determination take hold of her. She felt her heart speed up, beating blood strongly through her body. The sensations were welcome, she felt more alive in that moment than she had done in months. "You can't kill me. I will survive. I will carry on. I will live and I will love again" she thought.

She knew that for a new, joyful, wiser Cara to be born, first the old Cara needed to die completely, in all its existing shapes, forms and colours. For the old Cara to die, she needed to get away from the poison of this place. The poison that numbed and suffocated her. The biting harsh bitterness of her mother that kept taking pieces of her soul and destroying her life.

She felt content for the first time in months. She had a mission, an aim, a purpose. And her purpose in life was to re-find life and joy. Her purpose was to make it through this dark night, heal her heart, to find strength in her experience and love in her pain and reach a better place inside and out.

What was the dream again? It must have been powerful. No details remained, just the feelings and thoughts it had left behind. And those were enough. They were the gifts of her dream. They had been left behind for her to take heart from, to be guided by. Cara whispered a gentle thanks to the dream fairies.

She remembered an image from her past, something about getting lost, going to the wrong place, losing her purpose. And it came to her. She had set out to see a friend, someone she had met, liked and trusted while she was away. She had set out to see him, knowing he would comfort her and give her pearls of wisdom and confidence as he always did. But she had lost her way. She got distracted, got on the wrong horse, turned down the wrong path, followed the wrong star. She struggled on, trying to find her friend, and at times forgetting completely why she had set out on the journey in the first place. The image was full of confusion, losing again and again her way and her purpose, but continuing nonetheless. Even when she could not remember where she was going and why, she kept moving on. And this was the image she needed to hold on to. She needed to move. It did not matter that she didn't know where she was going. It did not matter what she would come across. It did not matter that her chance of survival was low. The only thing that mattered was that she kept moving, on and on, further into the darkness to find light eventually, even if through sheer coincidence.

She saw once lush lands, forests and rivers all cemented over. Nothing grew in those once wild lands any more. It had all been turned to grey cement, completely ruined. All life destroyed. Not a weed, not a bird left behind.

She wondered how she had ended up there. How could she have set out for paradise and ended up in a place of death, no sign of life, of nature or beauty. That wasn't paradise. Where had she gone wrong? How had she been so mislead?

The answer would come once she was alone. She would find the answer. She would search and walk until she found the answer. There was no point gradually moulding away here. A slow, numb death. Here, she would go mad before she could die. She needed to move, to search, to find and understand. She wanted to learn again, find new places, see different things. She had to leave this mouldy, rotten life of hers behind. Like a snake shedding its skin. Like spring shoots budding out of dark, cold ground. She needed to move on, leave everything she knew behind, let go of old ways, old friends, old loves and memories. Her current way of being needed to die completely.

She remembered her confusion in the dream. Not knowing what the point of her journey was. There was so much confusion around where she had wanted to go and where she had ended up. The dream and the image were linked. Perhaps they were one and the same, different realisations of the same root truth.

They both linked into where she was in her life at that very moment, how she felt and lived her current life. She felt confused about who she was, her role in life, what to do next, the right and helpful direction to take, the right and good decisions to make. She felt trapped and lost. She had no idea which way to turn. She could not even have asked for directions, as she had no idea where her destination was or what to ask, or whom to ask. She did not know what to wish for, to hope for, to pray for. She was in the middle of a blank canvass. Except the canvas was black and she held no brush and had no paint. Just infinite black all around.

If she stayed here, she would continue in confusion, decaying gradually as she stood on hold, waiting without knowing what she was waiting for. She had to move. Stagnation brought death. Nothing came to those who spent their lives waiting. But those who were active, who actively went out into the world and searched, and looked, those who asked questions even when they didn't understand what they were asking and why and listened to answers that were at times mute or spoken in foreign tongues, those were the ones who eventually found their questions and the matching answers. They were the ones who found the signs and markings along the path to guide their way, spilt paint to use with their fingers, moments of light to provide guidance. She needed to be active, to at least try to find a solution. Danger and painful death would be better than this slow rotting from the inside she was experiencing.

She didn't think she had the energy or will to make it far, but she had to try, she had to force herself to take the first step. Once that was done, there would be no turning back. What could be worse than how she felt right now anyway? Nothing. Nothing at all. A gang of evil men along her route could not hurt her as much, or cause her as much suffering as the man she held dearer than anyone or anything in the world had done. There was nothing in the world she feared. The worst had happened and she was still alive. What chance did anyone else have of hurting her? And if she died, how blissfully welcome that death would be.

She was ready. She felt impatient even. A mini spark in her months of darkness. And that was all she needed. That mini spark would get her out. And once out, she would have to move on. Just like she had continued with all her duties and chores, mindlessly, monotonously in her village, once out there she would have to keep moving on. She knew she could do it. And she knew she had to do it right now, before the strength and will left her once again, before she was lost in that nothingness she had grown so used to, unable to care for or want anything. She had to leave right now.

She felt tired.

She gazed blankly at her belongings. There were so few of them. Just a few items of clothing, a clay bowl, some stones and a bracelet he had given her. She gently picked up the bracelet, as if it were fragile and might crumble away in her fingers. She imagined she were touching his face.

The bracelet was strong, a row of solid, different coloured stones. Unlike his feelings for her, which had not held the strength and durability of these little stones, nor the vibrancy of their colours. She held it tightly in her fist, willing his energy, his touch to pass into her through the bracelet. She wanted desperately to feel him in her body. She felt her yearning for him rage up inside her and her thoughts call out to him, full of love, hope and hopelessness. She closed her eyes and imagined him stopping abruptly in his tracks, feeling a cold shudder pass through his body. The cold drawing his attention to the gaping hole her absence had created in his heart, in his life. She willed him to realise that hole was left there by her absence and that the only way he would feel whole, happy, warm again was if he rode right back and gathered her in his arms, never again to part from her, never again to want to leave her even for a moment.

An anguished cry left her chest and rasped out through her lips. She shuddered and tried to shake herself back into reality. But she had no strength. She lay down on her bead, silent tears flowing down her cheeks. Immobilised in body, frozen, she felt dead. She passed out from sheer exhaustion and grief.

It was still the middle of the night when she came to again. Her sister had draped a blanket over her cold body while she slept. She gathered the blanket around her as she rose. The night was so quiet, it was as if the entire outside world had vanished suddenly or stopped still or died. It was cold, inside, outside, throughout her body. She grabbed a scarf and threw a few items of clothing on it, then she wrapped the scarf around her few items and tied it in a firm knot. She gazed at her bracelet, determined to say goodbye to it. She found she was not able to. She let go of angry thoughts towards herself for being so weak and all feeling of sadness and loss as she slipped her hand through it. It felt good on her wrist, solid and safe. She wasn't ready to say goodbye yet. That day would come, she assumed, some day. No point forcing it, she assured herself. She did know that her earlier yearning and willing would give no results, he would not return for her. It was possible that he had already forgotten her and someone else was warming his bed and preparing his food. Again her heart screamed with the thought and again she pushed it away from her mind.

She tiptoed out of the room, into the cold, clear, dark night. She decided she would enter the desert. She didn't expect to survive for long. Some form of death would surely find her there. It was odd though. As welcome as the thought of death was, she still drew her blanket in closer around her body and filled her flask with water from the well, she still had a natural instinct to provide warmth and life for herself. Why, she could not understand. What kept people going, kept them struggling to stay alive, when there was nothing left to live for? If she was so desirous of dying, why bother with these details and delay her time of death by a day or two?

She let these thoughts pass, curious, yet not that interesting. As yet she had no answer. They were beyond her comprehension and anyway, she had hardly any strength left in her. All she knew for certain was that she needed to be far, far away , as far away as at all possible from her village by day break. She did not want to be found or saved. She wanted solitude and death to find her in quiet isolation, when she was alone at last, out in the wilderness. Alone with her grief and pain.

The sand was cool and gently yielding under her feet. She welcomed the sensation of her feet sinking into the sand as she walked on. That sensation felt far more real to her than her entire life had felt since she had returned to her village.

The sky was dark except for the moon and hundreds of stars. They shone brightly, unburdened by the sorrows and pains of this world. She gazed at them wistfully. Why could she not be a star, shining brightly, no shadows, no darkness, forever light. They offered her enough light to walk by. It didn't really matter if she saw her way anyway, she had no idea where she was going or what direction to walk in. She had no path, no route, no aim, no guide, no direction and no destination. It really did not matter which way she went.

For a moment, the sparkling stars seemed happy to her, as if they were dancing and singing. She wished they would sing to her, guide her with their songs. She could not have felt alone with the stars by her side. But the moment passed and even the stars turned cold towards her. They were too far. They were frozen in the dark sky. They passed no message onto her, gave her no warmth and showed no guidance.

All she had on her side was the cold night air she felt against her skin, penetrating her clothes, the dry cool sand under her feet and the desolation and dark emptiness she felt in her heart. She felt her tears all the way back in her stomach. They were nowhere near the surface. They were stuck so far within her, they could not release.

She walked on and as day started to break, the cold began to ease. Her legs felt tired, her feet were aching, but she continued. She walked on for another couple of hours. Gradually the heat grew intense. The sun was burning her, relentless, absolute, punishing rays of heat, dry, harsh, strong, unyielding, certain and forceful. The heat not only came down on her directly from the sun, but also rose up to her from the sand. She knew she would not be able to continue for much longer. She needed a place to rest. She looked around her hoping to find some shelter, a friendly growth or even a small sand mound offering a bit of shadow maybe. But nature had nothing to offer her as far as her eyes could see. She continued a little more. The thought of lying in the sun unsheltered was worse than moving on. She knew she'd fry to death if she lay down where she was.

Just as she was thinking she could not take a single step more, she saw a mound ahead of her. She dragged her tired, stiff legs towards it and lay down with her back against its rise. It offered a little shelter, and as small and insufficient as that was, she was grateful for it. She expected little and asked for even less. She covered her head with her scarf. She felt she had done all she could to protect herself. As she lay there she knew she didn't really care what happened to her. She left herself to the gods and lost consciousness quickly, fatigue and heat taking over her body and darkness invading her mind.

The dragon

Cara woke up with a start. She felt confused at first, surprised at her unfamiliar surroundings, the excessive heat pounding down on her, the monotonous desert stretching out around her in all directions with no sight or change disturbing the gold stretch of unending sand and clear blue sky. She had no idea how long she had been sleeping for. The sun had moved a little lower in the sky, so perhaps two or three hours. She was thirsty and dry, but she needed to ration her water, she didn't have much left as it was. She felt a little nauseous and her brain was banging against her skull, her head throbbing viciously. The excessive heat, sun and lack of water were taking their toll.

She remembered what had woken her up so suddenly. She had dreamt of a calcium dragon, demanding attention by growing ever larger as she watched it. It had been hissing and she understood its language, words spoken directly into her brain: "You need to know me, I am your guide". Its huge head looming ever larger and ever closer, taking over all space.

She could not ignore the message, although she did not quite understand it. What was this dragon? A mythical animal that didn't really exist. An animal alive, hissing, communicating, yet created out of calcium, a cold mineral, not living tissue, or flesh. She wondered about the myths and stories of dragons. She thought her answer might lie within those tales. At that moment she could not remember any though. All she could remember was that dragons brought death and destruction wherever they went. They loved shiny objects, gold and precious stones and searched them out, stealing what caught their eye. Their weapon was that they breathed out fire.

How was she to find this dragon and get to know it? Would it not eat her or burn her, or both, whatever dragons did to people. She had certainly never heard of a good dragon or one that gave humans any guidance.

Where was she to look for an understanding? She had no idea. She felt deep inside of her that she had to follow the dream's wisdom. She had to find the dragon to receive its guidance and the only action available to her at that moment was to go on. If it was meant to be, she would find it. She would be guided in the right direction. Her role was to keep going and not to give up. Guidance would come, if she continued her journey. Maybe the stars would help her tonight.

She walked on in searing heat for what felt like hours, but the sun was moving slowly and she knew she hadn't been walking for as long as her throbbing head and aching legs told her she had. As slow as its movement was, Cara was grateful that the sun was moving lower on the horizon. She was looking forward to the dark cool of night. The thought of feeling cold didn't seem as bad as it once had to her. She welcomed approaching night with its cold air and soothing darkness. Even freezing would be fine. Anything but this oppressive, burning heat.

She stopped at one point, too tired to continue. She didn't have much water left, but she needed to drink. She felt a sinking in her heart as she finished the last few drops remaining in her flask. The heat was too relentless, her throat too dry, her legs too tired. She felt dizzy from fatigue and the heat. Her skin was burning, her eyes stinging. "I can't continue", she thought, "I simply can't go on. I've had enough. I don't have the strength. I don't even want to anymore. I don't care what happens to me, I just want to lie down". She forced herself to take a few more steps, but it was pointless, she simply didn't have any strength left in her. She collapsed to the ground and passed out.

Dreams visited her again in her sleep. They were confused, blurry, unclear, full of anxiety and panic. In one dream she kept running from who knows what, but she never got away from whatever was pursuing her. It was an endless race. She managed to remain a few steps ahead, just enough to stay out of her pursuers reach, but she never could increase the distance between them. She could not stop for breath or rest. She had to keep running, forever just a few steps ahead of death, only a few steps, never less, never more. The fear and panic and need to get away enveloping her like a heavy dark cloak. Whatever was pursuing her was close behind, she could feel its presence, but she could never see it. It didn't catch up with her, but it never lost ground either. Running endlessly on an on.

Another dream brought the dragon back "Get to me", it hissed, "you have to get to know me". "How?" she screamed at it, "where are you, how do I find you", but the dragon had vanished.

In one dream there was mist everywhere, so thick she could not see beyond her nose. She was groping around in its blank grey, her arms stretched forward, searching for something solid to hold on to. She had no idea where she was or which way to go. Nothing solid offered itself to her grasping hands. They remained empty and searching.

She woke up with a start. She understood the first and last dreams. She was lost, blind in darkness, in both dreams, just as she was now in reality. There was no way out for her, her actual surroundings were too dark to see in. There was no path, no light, no life, no guide. She could not see what was around her and she could feel panic. Groping and searching blindly. But the dragon, she still did not understand, she could not guess.

The sun had gone down behind the horizon, the air was already slightly cooler. Stars had appeared in the black sky. She welcomed the sight of dark sky, glittering with stars, droplets of hope and light scattered all around. The cool air was relieving to her heated, tight nerves. She looked up at the stars, but her mind was so frantic, she could not see their patterns. Her mind had gone blank to all knowledge, to everything Tenzin had taught her. They made no sense to her, they would not communicate, they refused to guide her and her mind refused to calm down. She felt her sense of confusion increasing and a feeling of desperation grew in her heart. She closed her eyes.

"Dear God, please, please help me. I'll die, willingly, if that's what You wish, I would welcome death. But if You mean me to stay, please show me the way, please calm my mind, send me a sign, please"

She felt her breath moving in and out of her body, fast and shallow at first, but as she continued to watch, it slowed down. She could feel her heart becoming calmer. She opened her eyes. She could see the stars now. She searched for an answer, for some guidance in them. One of them shone especially bright, catching her eye and holding her attention. She felt she needed to follow that one.

She got up slowly, her limbs had seized up during her rest and every part of her body ached. She willed herself to focus on her breath. She looked up at her chosen star and started walking towards it. "I need water" she thought, "I need water desperately and soon"

She kept walking, with the star guiding her slow steps. Her mind was empty, too tired and overworked to think any longer. Her legs moved on as if by their own accord. All feeling had left her body and heart. She felt like a ghost, travelling through hellish fires and winds, moving on, ever moving on, with no comfort or release, no joy, no hope of escape.

At times feeling returned to her otherwise numb legs, when they screamed in pain. Her muscles no longer wanted to obey her orders, her legs were ready to collapse. She found she didn't have the energy to make the decision to rest. Her mind struggled with any thought. She kept moving, rest elusive, her mind heavy, lacking understanding or any mastery over her body. She continued. "I'll rest when I collapse" she thought.

The stars were moving, their positions in the sky were changing. She knew time was passing, all be it dreadfully slowly. She was sure she would not survive another day in the heat, but she had lost all hope of finding shelter or water.

She could not be that far from her village and she knew of no settlements close her village. "Having no hope is the worst" she thought. "If I had hope, hope would give me energy and will, but I have none, not for tonight or tomorrow, and even worse, not for the rest of my life. Why am I doing this? Why don't I die? Why keep moving in a stale, unfair world, dragging my aching body and tired soul through days and years that can bring me nothing but pain, all hope gone, all potential dead? Let me go"

As her despair and weariness rose, her body hurt more, her steps grew slower. She knew she could not, must not give in to despair. Despair was her enemy, sucking life and soul out of her whole being. But she could not help it. It grew with every step she took. She tried to force it down, again and again. Eventually she gave up. She walked a few more steps with despair in her heart and pain throughout her body. Then she collapsed, unconscious, into darkness.

She woke up feeling much calmer. She felt comfortable, something soft and warm against her skin. She realised she was lying on a bed in a little hut. At first she thought she was back home, but her surroundings were not familiar to her. She wondered what her mother had done to the hut while she was away. Then, as her vision and mind cleared, she realised she was in a hut she had never seen before. For a moment she wondered if she had died and this was the location of her after life. Then she thought she must be dreaming, a welcome dream, unlike the previous ones of darkness, panic and death. This dream brought her comfort and peace and she wanted the feeling to linger on.

She turned her head towards a stirring sound and a light she saw flicker through the corner of her eye. There was an old woman crouching by a fire, stirring something in a heavy, large pot. Whatever she was stirring smelled good. Cara realised how hungry she was. She tried to swallow, but her mouth was too dry. Her throat locked up. She wanted to say something, but the effort overcame her. She closed her eyes once more. She could not tell what was real and what was dream.

It was dark when she came to again. Someone had placed a blanket over her body. She felt warm. The fire had died out. There were a few red ashes still glowing where it had once been, but no flame remained. Her surroundings had not changed. She gripped the blanket and her fingers clenched rough warm material. "This isn't a dream" she thought. "Where am I?"

She noticed she was able to swallow. Her throat no longer felt parched. Someone must have fed her water. She was grateful. She let herself drift back into a dark, dreamless sleep, her unanswered questions too tiring for her overworked, fatigued mind..

It was light when she next awoke. There were sounds all around her. She could hear people talking, footsteps, someone struggling under some heavy weight they were carrying. The fire was burning once again, with the same pot placed on it, but she was alone in the hut this time. She lay there, listening to the unfamiliar sounds made by a village awake and people going about their business. She wondered where she was, but it didn't matter. She felt safe. She knew she wasn't in her own village. She knew she wasn't dead. Those were the only things she needed to know at that moment. The rest would reveal itself in time and she was in no hurry to find out. Resting comfortably felt like such a luxury to her, she was content to stay as she was. Even her heart and mind were calm. There was an acceptance of her fate and a gratitude towards whomever had cared for her for the past day. Or had she been here longer?

She became aware of a sound at the entrance. Turning her head, she saw the old woman from the day before enter. The woman walked over to her and placed her palm on her forehead. She muttered softly and nodded her head. Her eyes were kind, her face wrinkled all over. She had rough hands, a sign of long years of hard manual labour. Cara closed her eyes again, still too weak to enquire. Her eyes ached and the effort of looking around was still too much for her.

The old woman walked over to the fire and reached up for a bowl from a shelf to its side. She poured some liquid from the pot into it and carried it over to Cara. She placed it on the floor by the end of the bed, then gently lifting Cara's shoulders and head, brought her to a sitting position. Cara opened her eyes, watching the woman's movements, feeling her kindness, her compassion and noticing her efforts to treat her gently.

The woman picked the bowl up with decisive, certain movements. There was no space for disagreement. Cara obeyed her movements. She started feeding Cara from the bowl. The liquid was dense with a taste of herbs Cara did not recognise. The texture felt good in her mouth and her throat welcomed the warm dense liquid. Already the first few mouthfuls brought warmth and colour back to Cara's cheeks. She felt life return back into her worn-out body.

She looked up at the kind woman and asked, hesitating slightly, "Where am I?"

The old woman smiled, a toothless smile "you're awake dear. You're in a deserted place, ignored by those who come across it and unheard of by any others. We're in the middle of the desert. This is the most isolated place in these forsaken lands. Even the gods forget about us often. But never you mind. You will recover. Drink some more"

Cara obeyed. It didn't really matter where she was anyway. She had followed the guidance of her star, so she must be where she was meant to be.

The night was already drawing in when Cara got up. She did not know how long she had been lying in that bed. She could not tell if she had been unconscious for days. She had no idea who had found her and how. She felt grateful for their help, the herbal brews, the comfort of the bed and warmth of the fire. She had a yearning to learn more, to find out why she had been guided to this place.

The hut was empty once again, so she stepped up to the entrance and looked around. She could see very few people around, only three of them. A man walking to her left in the distance with a dog at his heals, a girl playing with stones in front of a hut and a woman drawing water from a well.

The village was set in a circle, with the well in the centre. She could only see ten or so huts. There was no other sight or sound of people other than those three. She wondered where everyone was. And where was the old woman who had taken care of her? She sat to one side of the doorway and started to wait.

She felt calm. She was in no hurry. She did not yet know which direction she would walk in when the time came. She would have liked to have stayed for a few days, to rest and to get to know these people and familiarise herself with their way of life, but she could not depend on an old woman's kindness for too long. She could see their resources were limited. The huts were basic, although clean and tidy and the hut she had been staying in held very few items, only what was essential and no extras.

She could not see any lit fires or any light seeping out of the huts to suggest fires. Once again she wondered where everyone was. As far as she could see it was endless desert in all directions. Where could they have vanished to?

Then she saw them appear suddenly, seemingly out of thin air, from nowhere. They materialised in an instant a little distance away. A small group of people were walking towards the huts, not that far away. She could hear them now too, talking in hushed tones amongst themselves. Their sudden appearance confused her further. She hadn't dosed off or closed her eyes. How could she have missed their approach? There was nothing to hide their bodies. The desert stretched out endlessly, without any growth, any hills, nothing to prevent her from seeing them from much further away.

She let go of the struggle of trying to understand. Once again she thought "it doesn't matter", and waited patiently for them to reach the huts.

Once they reached the huts they dispersed, each moving towards their own home. Soon sounds of evening preparations started to rise out of the silence, the movement of objects, the lighting of fires, pans being filled and placed, vegetables being chopped. Hushed chatter, some laughter, at times a raised voice. She wondered what they ate and where they found their food. She could see no vegetation around at all.

The old woman walked up to the entrance and looked down at Cara where she sat. "you followed the star" she said. "Yes" said Cara, by this time beyond questioning anything, even the oddness of the situation and the old woman's ability to read her mind. She did not have it in her to follow the wonder in her heart, how could the old woman possibly know? The old woman emanated a sense of wisdom and kindness and Cara felt safe in her presence and accepted her knowledge. She trusted the woman naturally, easily, without doubt or questions.

The old woman smiled at her and walked into the hut. Cara sat on for a few more minutes, dazed, but serene. She could hear the hustle and bustle of evening preparations from the other huts and there was something very comforting about these familiar sounds and rituals. The sense of comfort came from the familiarity of what was being done and the ease with which she had been accepted in this alien place. She did not feel like she was amongst strangers. She felt a sense of satisfaction within her, she had made it. She had managed to get away from the poisonous atmosphere of her village. She had survived the first and most difficult part of her journey. She was free. This was all new, yet somehow not completely foreign.

Eventually she got up and walked in. The old woman was crouched by the fire as before, lighting it as Cara walked in. There were a few vegetables on the bench to the side of the hut. She must have brought them in with her. Cara was sure they weren't there before. She didn't recognise the vegetables, but they did not look exciting. They were all the same bland greyish colour, although each had its own different unique shape. There was a knife nearby and without being asked, Cara went over to the bench and started chopping them. She wanted to help the woman and needed to make herself useful.

The old woman didn't seem to notice, she continued on by the fire. Once it was lit, she used a metal stick to stir the ashes and fan them back out. Then she gazed at them thoughtfully with intent concentration. "She's reading the ashes" thought Cara. She had heard it could be done, but had never met anyone who knew how to until now.

She felt her curiosity rise. So essential this blessing of curiosity, stirrings of life in her chest awoken by it, a faint interest in life, bringing with it tiny tastes of forgotten sources of joy. It had been a long time since she had last felt interested in anything and she welcomed the sensation. A realisation struck her, "Feeling alive is finding interest, being curious and constantly learning and growing" she thought. She was grateful to feel alive again, no matter how faint the feeling was. She smiled as she chopped away.

Her reverie was interrupted by the old woman's worn, but kind voice "I will teach you" she said. Even this sudden reading of her mind did not surprise Cara, nor this woman's intention to take her under her wing. She would teach her. She had already saved her life, given her a bed, warmth, water and food. Yet none of it surprised Cara. It all felt natural and right at that moment. "Yes", she thought, "yes, I would like that. I understand why the star led me to you and you understand why I have been led here too".

Cara settled into a comfortable routine. The old woman was called Rinchen. She reminded Cara of Tenzin and her heart warmed to her from the start. Rinchen had a laid back, easy going attitude and was calm, relaxed and settled in her way of living. She was never in a hurry and she did not seem to have any concerns or worries. She took everything, every duty, every circumstance, each rising and setting sun, each different season and all that life brought her with a calm, easy and level attitude. She was respectful of nature, nature's movements and messages. She gave thanks for each gift it bestowed on her, no matter how small what she received was. She watched her surroundings with interest. She had about her the air of someone who is at peace with the world and their place in it.

Her movements were level, grounded, calm and relaxed. Her voice was authoritative yet gentle, a voice that gave the person hearing it a desire to obey and listen. Cara eased into the slower pace of her life with her quickly. She helped Rinchen whenever she could. Rinchen never asked or told Cara to do anything, but as soon as Cara noticed her taking on an activity, she went to her assistance without any need for words or guidance. They settled into an easy companionship with reciprocal support and understanding.

Most of Cara's duties were straight forward. She pulled water out of the well every morning and lit the fire twice a day, first thing and as the sun set. She chopped vegetables and prepared brews. After breakfast she cleaned the hut and tidied away blankets.

Even after a few days of this simple routine and living with Rinchen, Cara was still not able to say where the wood for the fire or the vegetables for the brews or the medicinal herbs that kept appearing on the bench daily came from. Every afternoon, a couple of hours before sun set Rinchen would leave with the other villagers, returning only when the sun had disappeared beyond the horizon and the sky was losing its light. Cara could make no sense of it and it seemed to her nothing short of a miracle, yet they all returned with a few vegetables and enough wood for the evening and morning every single day.

Their meals, twice a day, were always exactly the same. In the evening she prepared bland vegetables and stewed them in the large pot and in the morning they had the leftovers from the night before, reheated over the morning fire. She never saw any other food, and no event or incident ever seemed to change the set routine.

Although the vegetables they ate essentially remained the same, Rinchen did bring with her different varieties of herbs each day. There was ever changing mixtures of them and whenever she brewed some up she would call Cara to her, show her the herbs, freshly picked, explain what they were, how they were grown and what use they had. Then she showed her how to prepare them. She must have been some kind of village doctor, for she had a herb for every ailment or need that the people had and preparing these herbs and seeing to the villagers health took up most of her time and energy.

Cara was still drinking the herb mixture Rinchen had fed her on her first day in this village daily. She had learned that it built strength, not only of the body, but also of the heart, a remedy Cara needed more than anything.

There was never any idle talk between them. Rinchen did not ask where she had come from or why. Cara did not wonder at this much. She thought Rinchen might already know the answers in her unique, wise way.

Day by day Cara felt life return back into her being. She was able to rise in the mornings feeling lighter, carrying less of all that darkness in her heart. She could go about her chores with enough awareness of her surroundings and consciousness of mind to notice details and take in sights. She was keen to learn and to please. Interest in life and all it had to offer was being renewed in her daily and that gave her the energy and will to live. She did not feel light hearted or happy yet, but even this amount of movement within her was more than she had expected a few months before. She realised time and life itself would eventually heal even the deepest of her wounds. It astounded her that such a thing was possible, but her own life and days were testament that time had its own power and with the help of nature, it healed every wound, no matter how deep and bad, eventually.

She also realised with each day that she had so much more yet to learn. The fountain of new knowledge could never dry up and as long as she kept an interest in learning, her life would be worth living. Learning and serving gave her an aim, something to do, a way to live and they fed her soul with pure vitality.

One evening soon after the fire had burned itself out, Rinchen called Cara over to her. She started stirring the ashes, the way Cara had seen her do before. Cara watched. She wanted to ask if there was a method in her stirring. She wanted to ask many questions, but she had already learned during her short time there that Rinchen followed her own timing. She could not be rushed or forced into changing her rhythms. Cara knew she would find out everything she needed to when the time was right for Rinchen.

Cara was staring at the embers, trying to see something, whatever it was that Rinchen saw, focusing hard, trying to understand. She saw nothing but ash and a few bits of wood still burning red. She gazed up at Rinchen, who was studying them quietly. She waited.

"You see nothing child" she said after a while. Cara shook her head. "Patience. Youth is impatient. Learn patience. Learn to trust the rhythm and the laws of nature. Learn to wait patiently. Be calm. Still your mind. Slow your breath and your heart and you will see all". Then she got up and walked away.

Cara remained at her place staring intently at the remains

of the fire until there was nothing left to stare at and no light to see by. She had seen nothing, felt nothing, understood nothing.

She went to bed, annoyed with herself for failing, feeling frustrated and angry. Eventually she fell asleep.

She woke up in the middle of the night with Rinchen's voice ringing in her ears, repeating "be patient, still your mind" over and over again. She sat up, expecting to see Rinchen by her side, but she was not near here. She was fast asleep on the other side of the hut. Cara lay back down and closed her eyes, puzzling over the experience. She was just about to doze off again when she understood. She had tried too hard when gazing into the embers of the fire. She had been too wilfull. She had tried to force nature, not wait for it. She fell asleep content and relieved.

Over time Cara did learn to read the dying embers of a fire. Or rather, she learned to open herself up to what the embers had to offer. She practised every night until one evening she saw an image. She saw a dragon in the ashes, a red glow in its thick, long neck. She had stumbled across her dragon once again, or more probably, it had found her. She gazed at the dragon, wondering what it wanted to tell her, but it communicated nothing. At least nothing Cara could understand.

The next evening Rinchen came in with a young woman by her side. When they came in, Cara was sitting by the dying fire as usual, gazing at it intently, waiting for its images and messages to materialise, to become clear to her as yet novice eyes.

Rinchen brought the woman to Cara's side and said "You are ready. Read for her". Cara felt a moment's hesitation. She didn't feel ready, she had no confidence at all in her ability to read, but Rinchen had told her to. She felt she had to obey and she wanted so much to please her teacher.

She looked at the young woman for a few minutes, letting the woman's energy seep into her, trying to feel into the woman's soul and heart, trying to read her eyes and listen to her breath. She felt the presence of a sadness in the woman. And yet her face showed no emotion. There was a mismatch in what Cara felt from the woman and what the woman communicated willingly to her surroundings. "Don't get influenced by her calm, serene look" Cara told herself, "remember the people in your village, their faces immobile and cold. No emotion can be read in their faces either, yet their bitterness, their helplessness and anger is palpable to anyone who stops to pay attention for a moment".

Cara stirred the ashes for a few moments. Then she focused on her breath, watching it slow down as she watched it. Once her heart was calm, she gazed at the ashes and started to wait, asking for guidance, praying gently inwardly, without urgency. She knew she was only a messenger. She did not create the images or work them out herself. She had to wait for them to be gifted to her. A gift can not be demanded or rushed. Eventually the vision came. She saw a burial ground and a cloud of grief surrounding it. She asked in her prayers "how can I help her?" and waited once more.

Some time had passed and Cara started to feel afraid that the answer would not come to her. She was afraid of letting Rinchen down. She was afraid of no words, no guidance coming to her and the quiet emptiness in the room surrounded her chest and heart as the fear set in. She looked up at Rinchen, feeling nervous, but Rinchen was smiling at her with confidence and her confidence gave Cara courage. She looked back at the ashes and saw a young man. He was leading a camel. She felt he had travelled a great distance. He was smiling and carried his body with a lightness and ease. Neither the distance he had travelled, nor the heat, nor the weight he was carrying seemed to burden him.

She looked up at the woman and said "you will meet a young man who will travel here from far away. He will come with a camel and lots of wisdom. His teachings will bring lightness to your heart. Listen to him and allow yourself to be guided by him".

She looked at Rinchen, who nodded and led the young woman back out of the hut. Cara felt a surge of joy. She felt excited, her cells tingling with life. She marvelled at the feeling, a feeling that she had thought she had lost forever, one she had not felt for so long. She had forgotten what joy felt like. She knew what she had told the woman was the truth. She felt it. She also felt that Rinchen was pleased with her. She had been useful, she had been a messenger, a conduit for higher truths to reach a kindred spirit. And most importantly she had proved herself worthy of Rinchen's attentions, teaching, guidance and faith in her.

That night Cara dreamed of the desert and the burning sun. It was as harsh and relentless as it had been before, but it was calling to her. It was no longer her enemy. It had become her path, her route and current destination. She knew she needed to walk on through it. She needed to understand its ways and learn from its wisdom.

When she woke up she knew the time had come. She loved Rinchen and had become comfortable in her life with her. She did not want to leave, but she knew she had to. She could not stay in a comfort zone, forgetting her calling to learn and understand. If she stayed she would stagnate and soften in an easy life. She had yet to travel. She had found a short respite, enough to rekindle her interest in life and learning and her faith in human beings and God. She had received enough nourishment to feed her body and soul, just enough to prepare her for the next phase of her journey. But this was not the end, there was more and she had to go out and meet it.

She was grateful. Her most important lesson had been to experience how time changes all feelings, how even the worst and most deadly wounds can eventually heal and how her spirit had not been killed and could not be suffocated forever. She would remember this lesson. It would support her when she felt despair return to her. If she felt all hope lost, her life covered in darkness, she would remember that light was everywhere and its rays would reach her eventually, no matter how unbelievable that might seem at that moment.

Fear had left her and so had despondency and depression. She felt stronger in her body, mind and heart. She felt determined to continue. She felt gratitude and love towards Rinchen and promised herself to always keep her in her heart and prayers and bring her back in to her mind whenever she felt herself falter with doubt, when she lost the will to go on or lost interest in life. There would always be more amazing people to meet and learn from, further interesting things to find out and experience. Always a new experience around the corner to rejuvinate her soul. And Rinchen's image would serve to remind her of that.

When Cara returned to the hut with water, she saw something laid out on her blanket. She walked over and saw that it was some kind of square shaped rough material that you could fold into a satchel. Laid inside were a flask of water, some cooked vegetables, a blouse and a scarf. Rinchen had known what she had seen her dream and the decision it would bring with it, just as she always knew the most important things in advance. She had made her own preparations for Cara's departure. Once more Cara felt grateful for her thoughtful acts of kindness. Her gentle, loving goodbye filled Cara with warmth and she felt comforted by the knowledge that she did not need to explain anything. It was all okay and everything was happening in the way it should be.

Cara set off after she finished her morning chores and shared a last breakfast with Rinchen. She hesitated on her way out, glancing back at the space that had been her home for the past few months and the woman who had been her friend, guide, teacher and mother. Rinchen smiled at her. Cara knew, as she had known so many times before, that Rinchen understood her, truly and fully. She was glad her feelings were known to Rinchen. She would not have known how to put them in words and this saved her the effort and the possibility of misunderstanding. Rinchen's understanding glance gave Cara support, a feeling of connection and friendship in this vast, lonely, hostile world. She knew their connection would last through time and over any distance she might cover.

Cara wanted to hug her, but there was something about the way Rinchen held herself that forbid physical shows of affection or any outbursts of emotion. Instead Cara bowed her head and kissed Rinchen's hand. Then she placed her right hand over her own heart as a symbol of the gratitude and love she felt. She wandered off in the direction Rinchen was gazing.

Cara didn't dare turn back until she had walked for a good fifteen minutes. When she eventually did look back, the village seemed small and insignificant in the wide, broad horizon. She felt sad leaving, but knew she had to. She was only at the beginning of her journey. Having come close to death and complete despair, and survived them through seemingly nothing but chance and nature's will, Cara walked with more confidence this time. She trusted she would be provided for and whatever she needed for her journey, as long as she kept going, searching and seeing, would be given to her. She knew also that she would be given nothing more than that which was absolutely essential for her survival. Growth, learning and wisdom would come to her through hardship and struggle, not through ease and comfort. There were no short cuts or easy ways. As long as she played her part, there would always be a guiding star or a helping hand to keep her moving forward.

Cara's faith in her journey, in the wisdom of nature and the will of the universe was strong enough to give her will and energy and she walked on enjoying the solidity of her renewed confidence. Her heart was lighter than when she had set out from her own village. She felt stronger.

The sun was a bright haze in the sky, immense, a burning ball consuming all within its reach. Cara pulled her scarf close over her head and shoulders, trying to create as much shelter for herself as she could. Without knowing where she was going and how she would get there, Cara walked on.

She reached an area where all around her she could see many scattered sand dunes. She decided it might be a good place to take a break and sat behind a dune, in shelter from the setting sun. She closed her eyes, feeling weary from her long walk and the intensity of the heat.

As soon as she was asleep, her dragon materialised in her mind. It was already much larger than last time and it was growing in size as she watched it. At first appearance, only the dragon's head was visible. It was as big as the whole of Cara. Its size and strength were daunting. As Cara watched, the dragon's head continued to grow, until Cara had to back away. Any closer and she would have been consumed by the dragon. Some white substance, like solid calcium was pouring out of the dragon's mouth, as if the dragon was spewing eggs of calcium, and it was from this calcium that its head was growing larger. The dragon was made of this calcium like substance. Calcium pouring out, solidifying and adding to the already monstrously large head.

The dragon stretched its long, thick neck towards Cara and roared menacingly. No fire came out of its mouth, just smoke, as if the fire in its belly had gone out and these were the last breaths of a dying creature. She felt the dragon's hot breath on her face and with it, its rage. She was afraid the dragon would consume her or kill her. It was certainly capable of swallowing her whole. But she wondered what a dragon was without the ability to spew fire? What was this calcium it was made of? Why was the calcium cold, while the dragon's breath was hot?

She woke up with a start, puzzled. She had felt all along that she needed to get to know the dragon, that the dragon would provide her with the answers to her questions. But how could she get to know such a vicious, angry monster? How could she even get close enough to it without getting killed? And why did the dragon have no fire? Her dream came with a feeling of war. She needed to fight the dragon. How could she both fight it and get to know it at the same time? How could she fight it without dying? What did the dragon symbolise? What was she meant to fight and what was she meant to understand?

She closed her eyes once more and prayed. The answer was not going to come from her own mind, she needed guidance. Rather than answers, the dragon was bringing her more questions.

She heard a voice in her head "Every being has a weak spot". She understood. To kill an animal, you need to find its weak spot. To find the weak spot, you need to first get to know it. The dragon had an outer layer of calcium shell, solid, impenetrable. She could not get through to its inner living material, if there was any, through its shell. But if she found its weak spot and struck a blow there, she could kill it. And to know the dragon's weakness, she needed to get to know the dragon first.

Cara gathered her bag and started walking once more. She wanted to cover as much distance as she could before darkness set in completely.

As she walked, Cara thought about the dragon, bringing back the image from her dream to her mind. The dragon was aggressive, it was an attacker. It was threatening and menacing.

It inspired fear in others. What did that symbolise? She thought of her mother. The rage with which the dragon had come on to her was like a replay, a symbol of the rage her mother felt towards her and the world in general. Her mother's rage lacked flame too. Her hiss brought forward smoke without fire. She felt that the path to understanding the dragon was one and the same path as understanding her mother.

Her mother too was full of hatred and anger, hot and burning. And yet at the same time the fire inside her had died. She no longer had life energy. She was frozen solid. She had lost the ability to burn. She was menacing and threatening and yet she had caused Cara no physical harm. She had inflicted on Cara only the freezing poison of her hatred. She had not been able to destroy Cara. Any harm that had come to Cara from her mother had been possible only because Cara had allowed her to hurt her.

She let go of the thought. She had learned that answers usually came when her mind was quiet and empty, not when she was frantically searching for them. Answers could not be forced into her consciousness, they appeared when they wanted to, when she was ready to receive them.

The sand was cooler under her feet and she welcomed the breeze that brushed her cheeks. It was getting dark, but the sky was clear. She would be able to continue by the light of the stars. She wondered if she would see the bright star that had led her to Rinchen so many months ago. That was no longer the star for her though, even if it did appear. She was grateful to it for lighting her way and guiding her to Rinchen's fire, but its role had been completed and she needed to find new guides towards new destinations.

Cara learned to survive in the desert. She could make use of cacti and weeds she came across, drinking their juice and finding nourishment in their fleshy parts. She came across little isolated inhabitations from time to time, where she found work for a few days in return for food. She didn't linger long in any one place though. She kept moving.

The one notable experience during the few months that followed was when she came across a snake near a gathering of weeds. The snake was shedding its skin. Cara seated herself nearby to watch. She found the way the snake moved fascinating. It was gradually worming itself out of its old, worn skin. The skin that appeared beneath was young, new, bright and shiny. It glittered in the sunlight.

Once the snake was rid of all its old skin, it lifted its head and hissed thrusting its pointy thin tongue out, then moved swiftly away out of her sight.

She continued to sit where she was long after the snake had left her. The snake had moved so naturally, so easily. Shedding old skin to bring forth the new, with all its freshness and symbolism of new life brought in to light. It symbolised her journey in a way. She had been shedding layer after layer of old skin ever since she'd left her home. Shedding old ways of being, thinking, living, believing. And with each step, each day and month, she was renewing herself by letting go of the old. She wondered how much longer she would have to travel before she had finished shedding all her old skin. She wanted to be able to move away into the distance with brand new shiny skin, with ease and lightness, unencumbered as the snake had done.

She shook her head and raised herself to continue her journey. There was no point thinking about how long, when and where. All she had at this moment was the journey and she needed to follow her path, for as long as it took, to wherever it led.

The silence and space of the desert gave Cara all she needed. The desert was unending. She could wander in it for lifetimes and still not reach an end. Bright golden sand as far as her eyes could see in all directions. Walking calmed her mind and heart. As she walked in this vast open space, she could feel and think and be, without anxiety, without burden or pressure. Thoughts passing through her mind, emotions rising and mellowing without rocking her soul out of its calm rhythm. She found comfort in the limitless space surrounding her and the ease that came from journeying alone, completely free and unhindered. Her spirit felt light and free and she cherished her long days of walking.

When thoughts or questions came to her mind, she pondered them for a while, then let go of them, releasing them into the warm air. She imagined the questions travelling upwards on the wind, moving vast distances much faster than she ever could. And once they found their partners, the matching answers, they returned to her, question and answer hand in hand. She let them find wholeness by setting them free, letting them float away. And in return, they showed off their new found other halves to her, sharing with her their wisdom.

Her dreams helped her too. Sometimes they brought her answers, but mostly they carried with them more questions to send out into the ether. When she needed guidance, she prayed and a reply came to her eventually, either in a dream, or in the twinkling of a star. Sometimes she saw the replies in the scarce vegetation she came across, or the odd animal that chose to hang around and communicate its message in its own way and language. As long as she was patient and didn't force or push nature's independent rhythm and the unique qualities of life's details, as long as she didn't try to control the outcomes or will them in a certain direction, all the answers and guidance she needed always came. eventually.

She found that quite often they waited until she was preparing to give up, or after she'd suffered a loss of heart for a while. It was as if the universe wanted to teach her faith and patience. It kept reminding her that despair never helped and that faith and perseverance were always rewarded. Each answer, each solution increased her confidence in herself and her path and that in turn increased her strength and lightened her heart. She was moving on and every day she felt a little better, a little wiser and a little stronger.

Her dragon was always in the back of her mind, lurking somewhere in the recesses. She knew she needed to understand the dragon's message to move further and deeper, but she didn't know how to communicate with it. And she didn't understand how defeating it fitted in with what she was searching for.

She thought of the dragon often, contemplating what it had already said and what her dreams had been telling her since. She sometimes brought its image back into her consciousness, watching it grow in awe, analysing its expression, its words, its movements.

The dragon was female, she was sure of that. Her mother had come to her mind when contemplating the dragon. Both dragon and mother are universal symbols of the feminine aspects of the universe. She felt that the path to understanding them had to lie through connecting to her own feminine side.

Tenzin had told her once that the feminine knew how to listen, hear and wait, to feel and accept, to understand and learn. The feminine allowed nature to take its course and knew how to flow with it, without resisting or fighting it. The feminine was the sensual, feeling side of nature. It demanded patience and acceptance. The masculine side of universal energy was about doing, changing and working the will to create, move, even force when necessary. Cara had already experienced the futility of trying to force an answer when it came to deeper senses, emotions and matters of the heart. To succeed in life she had to work, change, be active, use her masculine energies. But to learn and grow, to understand her own hidden layers, her unconscious, to learn how to move in tune with nature, with universe, with God, she had to stop trying and doing, she had to listen and feel, she had to wait and accept and stop struggling against nature, her own nature as well as that of the bigger, wider universe. Her path lay through an accepting, feeling way. And her endless walking provided the perfect backdrop to this. The vast universe all around her and she, walking through it alone, and yet not alone because of her connection to all around her.

Cara could feel the struggle within her. She had learned in the riders' settlement and Rinchen's village the importance of letting nature have its way and learn from experiences as much as possible, cherishing the good, growing through the bad. But within her heart the anguish still continued. She still felt the pain of losing her son and the man she loved. Her soul lamented and her mind wanted to deny the existence of such unfairness and so much pain. She struggled to fight the pain and her fate. She had to fight not to hate or rage. She was afraid of her anger. She had kept it squashed down for such a long time. Whenever it raised its head a little, Cara panicked. Its sheer strength and force were too immense. She thought that if even a little part of it escaped out, it would rupture like a volcano and explode into the universe, destroying her and everything around her, perhaps the whole universe. At times her whole soul cried out to the universe in defiance and anger. She could not imagine how cherishing her loss, pain and anger could be possible.

Feminine was earth, nature. Nature gave and received, to and from all without discrimination. The rain did not choose who to shower with its blessing depending on how good or bad they had been. She had to learn to love and accept all with such equality, including the good and bad in herself.

Cara decided to prepare an offering for the dragon. Next time she reached some vegetation, she gathered a few plants and flowers and tied them together. She knelt down and prayed to her dragon, asking for her guidance and offering her gatherings in return. Then she lay down and waited, eyes closed.

The answer appeared in her mind. It came from her heart,

not from the outer world. Her heart told her "calcium burns inwardly without producing a visible fire. You need water for it to burn".

Cara obeyed. She got up once more and squeezed as much water as she could out of a cactus into a hollow stone and placed it by the plants. She lay down and closed her eyes once more. She fell asleep.

She could see the dragon, stretching its neck, its huge head moving towards her. It looked fierce, but not menacing. Cara did not flinch or draw back, she stood her ground, looking directly into the dragon's eyes. The dragon was constantly laying more and more calcium, growing in size, its head and neck already vast. There was no body attached to them that Cara could see, just a head and neck hanging in mid air, yet not floating either. They were secured as if bound to the earth through a solid, invisible body of force. Its head was as big as a bungalow by now.

"You have no fear" the dragon hissed.

"I do" said Cara, plainly. She felt terror throughout her body. It was only through pure determination and will power that she was standing her ground. She knew there was no point trying to escape. She needed to learn from the dragon, and for that she needed to face it. Running from the dragon would take her back into despair. Better die trying, than to be lost in darkness and ignorance.

"You have spirit, but you are burdened. Shed your burden"

"How?"

"Fire cleanses, water heals, acceptance and knowledge lead to understanding and gratitude. And eventually they all lead to forgiveness and love. When your hatred of yourself and your anger towards the universe has melted away, you will find I exist no longer"

"How do I do that?"

"Keep on your journey, keep learning. Be patient".

"I don't understand anything you're saying. How do I forgive and love that which is unforgivable and unloveable?

I am on this journey, I have been for a long time. Where am I going? How do I get there? When will it end?" Cara's anxiety that the dragon would not give her the solution she needed was pouring out of her in hot tears. She was begging the dragon. In her desperation she had forgotten all fear.

"That is not the way Cara. You hold too much resentment. You are too impatient and wilful. You can't fight the universe and demand answers from it. It does not help its enemies, only those who are its friends. You're resisting even your own resistance. Let it go"

The dragon vanished.

Cara found herself crying bitterly. She cried herself out until she had calmed down. She felt hollow and empty after her outburst. But she could not rest. She felt too activated and restless to stay still. She had to move on. She picked up her small satchel and walked on.

That night the dragon returned to her in her dreams. The dragon was hissing out smoke and words and Cara was floating amoungst them. Hearing the words and feeling them on her skin. At times she saw a word appear in the clouds. She could hold them if she liked. They were in the forms of objects floating around. Sometimes they were the fluffy texture of a cloud, sometimes hard, solid pieces, separate from the clouds.

She saw the word 'fire' float by and heard the dragon hiss "Fire is purification. Purify your soul from ego and desires". Then she tumbled backwards into the clouds of smoke, somersaulting a few times, feeling dizzy and confused.

She felt the words carry her as she sensed them on her skin "You're enjoying destroying yourself. You find comfort in blaming and hating yourself. You're digging a big, deep, dark hole in your soul that can never be filled through blame and anger. A hole like your mothers, growing darker, deeper and more poisonous. The hole can only be filled with forgiveness, acceptance and learning to love yourself. Acceptance and love are the key to healing".

She felt the presence of the devouring dragon. A hungry, insatiable dragon, eating all in its path and never reaching satisfaction, fulfilment or contentment. The presence of the devouring dragon transformed into the body of her mother, the devouring mother, the Death Mother. The Death Mother that demands life, that feeds on the lives of others, eating, eating, devouring, killing and yet never being able to find satisfaction. Nothing can fill her dark hole. Unmet demands, unfulfilled desires, hunger that cannot be satiated, frustration, bitterness, anger, hatred.

She felt the darkness of the Death Mother turn on her. She saw herself as a little girl, standing helpless, in tears with the dark cloud of her mother surrounding her, swallowing her whole. She felt the Death Mother's motive, her one desire; to destroy and kill, to take and leave noting behind.

She heard the dragon hiss "Name it, see it, bring it into the light so that it is no longer in darkness. Then it can no longer devour you from the inside. It will dry out and shrivel into nothing in the glare of the sun. The honest brutal glare of the sun".

She saw the sun appear and then a lake. Then a large rock in the middle of the lake and before her eyes branches started to grow upwards from that rock, sprouting leaves and flowers. Within minutes the tree was fully grown, reaching out with its branches in all directions. Branches laden with growth and green. "And with the sun and water grows the tree of life" she thought. A symbol of wholeness and inner peace.

She saw the dragon, laying calcium and a fire erupted out of the mounds of calcium, the fire burning off complexes, purifying the unconscious, lighting up what is hidden in the darkness of denial. Calcium that conceives fire within it, but is cold to the touch. A hidden store of fire, life slumbering within it, unseen. An untapped source of energy.

Rain drops fell onto the calcium and she felt heat rise out of the mound. She watched as the heat and internal fire purified the area. The air became pure and clean and light. She felt herself breathe deeply.

She saw a wounded animal appear. It was bleeding out of a deep, wide wound on its side. And she watched as the blood started to transform the animal's flesh, not only in and around the wound, but gradually all over. The animal transformed into a healthy, lively deer, with sparkling eyes and moist nose, healthy and happy. She felt the meaning in the words forming around her, "The wound carries the healing. It is the source and home of healing."

She heard the dragon hiss, "You win the battle by naming the enemy. Naming it means bringing it into awareness, into consciousness. Name the wound and thereby heal it. Let it breathe, let it see the sun. Don't cover it up or hide it, or cut it off."

With those last words the dragon vanished, the clouds floated away on a fresh, light breeze. The sky became clearer. The sun was shining down on her, but no longer overwhelmingly hot. It had become warm and gentle. The deer twinkled something akin to a smile, then turned around and skipped off into the distance, full of lively agility. It was free. Birds appeared amongst the leaves of the tree of life. Butterflies were flying from flower to flower.

The Death Mother was melting, one with lava, her darkness spreading and dissolving in the red glow, until she vanished completely. The air smelled fresh. Cara noticed herself take in a deep, full breath, her spirit rejuvenated, she felt calm and rested.

Towards dusk one day she reached a village. It was set around a small lake, so small it was more like a large puddle. She wandered into the village just as it was getting dark. There were only a few people around. The smell of fires burning and vegetables brewing wafted out of the huts. She looked around, her eyes searching for a kindly looking woman.

Nobody paid attention to her. In other villages her approach had been met by surprise and questioning looks. It was not normal for a woman to be travelling through the desert alone. Someone would usually approach her and she would ask them for food and shelter. But this time no one seemed to even notice her. She might as well have been a breeze passing through the village, invisible and barely perceptible, certainly not noteworthy.

She saw a young girl by the water side and approached her slowly. She did not want to scare the girl. But even when she was standing directly by the girl's side, the girl paid no attention to her. Cara touched her arm gently. The girl looked up at her with a blank look in her eyes. Cara asked if there was an old lady in the village who would trade her some food in return for labour. The girl continued looking at her with no expression on her face, just an unseeing, blank, vacant skull, with empty eyes and features. Cara tried again, this time motioning with her hands what she was asking for as best she could. The girl shrugged her shoulders, got up and walked away without hurry.

Cara sat down feeling a little bewildered. She had never been greeted in a village this way. Their total indifference confused her. She wondered if the water in the lake was drinkable. She was thirsty. She looked around, but didn't see anyone drawing water from it. She decided to wait until she was sure.

She got up and started walking towards the closest hut. A man was sitting at its entrance. She walked up to him and repeated her question, with both words and hand motions. The man stared at her, then turned his gaze back into the distance. Cara was even more baffled. She could not understand their attitude. Had they been unwelcoming or defensive even, she would have understood better. But to so completely ignore a stranger who had just walked into their village?

She went back to the lake and started watching. She wanted to see where they got their drinking water from. She could easily sleep outdoors and forgo the food she had been looking forward to, but she really needed water.

Gradually, as darkness closed in further, all the inhabitants retired to their respective huts and the open space was left empty. Cara felt alone suddenly. She felt tiny in a vast, unknown world. A world in which she felt lost. She realised she did not have sufficient understanding of its ways. She felt a sudden awe that she had survived so far. "I have been lucky" she thought. She smiled at the thought that occurred to her. Walking on her own in a vast empty desert she had hardly ever felt alone, but in the midst of these people she felt isolated and lonely. How funny that people brought her loneliness while empty space did not.

There was nothing to it, she made herself comfortable by the lake and settled down to sleep. The villagers would need to fetch their water in the morning and she would then be able to quench her thirst.

Her sleep was broken. Her resting place felt eerie. There were spirits she did not recognise the energy of around her. They were not friendly, yet not directly threatening either. Something about their energy felt out of place. The whole village and its people were odd. Something was not right.

She woke up just before dawn. Her dream was still vivid in her mind. It was screaming a warning. It told her she needed to get away from this place as fast as she could. Her whole body was crying out to her to leave now, immediately. She felt the presence of imminent danger.

She shook her head and told herself not to be so easily scared. "You're being silly Cara" she thought to herself, "just because you don't understand them, doesn't mean they are dangerous. They have ignored you, not threatened you". And yet she could not shake the warning off.

She got up and walked over to the lake. She gathered some water in her palm and smelled it. It had no smell. She decided to take the risk. She drank from the lake and filled her flask. Then she straightened out her clothes and slung her satchel over her shoulder. She was ready to move on, yet something held her back, a sense of curiosity. She hated unanswered questions. She wanted to understand.

"Risk ignoring the warning or face ignorance" she thought.

The village was so quiet, what danger could come to her? If they had wanted to hurt her, would they not have done it the previous night? Yet the warning in her heart remained uncalmed.

She looked up at the sky for guidance, but there were no stars. She took a few steps away from the lake, but some force stopped her from going on any further. She realised she could not leave. Her will and curiosity prevented her from doing so. She decided to sit down and wait for the village to awaken.

To her it felt like a long time had passed until she heard the first stirring sounds rise out of the huts. Gradually the odd person started to appear at hut entrances. She sat still, waiting. A few men gathered together by the lake and then wandered off in the direction of the sun. They paid no attention to her. Their eyes didn't even seem to notice her.

The little girl from the day before walked out of a hut and wandered slowly over to the lake. She washed her hands, but didn't drink. A woman walked out of a hut and wandered in the opposite direction to the men. And then there was silence again. The only living being she could see or hear was the little girl, playing with sand and water by the lake.

Cara walked over to the girl, with not much hope this time. The girl didn't look up. Cara sat next to her, watching the girl's motions. The girl showed no excitement, or joy. She looked like she was in a trance, her sight opening into other worlds, aware of other dimensions, but oblivious to this one, unable to see the material objects and beings around her. Her actions were mechanic. Cara thought the girl moved like a machine, not a human being.

Then Cara's head started to spin. She felt sick in her stomach. Her sight flickered. She could feel herself lose consciousness. Cara passed out by the lake. The girl continued playing with the sand. She had not noticed.

Cara came to with the sound of great commotion. It had grown dark already. She must have been unconscious for a whole day. She puzzled at that. How could she have passed out for so long? There was shouting and panic in the air. She could hear running steps all around her. Her head hurt and her body ached. At first she could not remember where she was. But slowly it all came back to her. The odd village, the unseeing villagers, feeling sick and dizzy, the little girl. She lifted her head with effort. She could see a huge blaze nearby, glowing red and yellow, stretching its long wavy neck towards the sky. She could see shadows running around between huts and people shouting in a language she did not understand.

She strained her eyes to try to see what was going on. A hut was on fire. It was burning so beautifully. Graceful flames licking the air around it. There was something so vibrant and alive about the fire, at first Cara simply marvelled at it, without really taking in its consequences. The red, orange and gold of the fire was awe inspiring. Cara watched the flames dance, mesmerised.

When she was able to look away again, it took her a few minutes to take in what was going on around her. She could not understand the actions of the villagers. There was water right there. Why were they not putting the fire out? Instead they were laying stones between the hut and the lake. Cara sat up, increasingly confused. The feeling of panic emanating from the villagers caught her too. She jumped to her feet, looking around for a bucket. "Why don't they put the fire out" she kept thinking. Her head was hurting and she still felt a little nauseous. She wasn't sure she was taking in her surroundings properly. She felt too confused, vague and dizzy to be sure of anything, or to be able to think a thought through to its conclusion.

There was a bucket near the entrance to a hut. She grabbed it and ran back to the lake, filling it with water. She started running towards the hut, but a man got in her way and pushed her to the ground. He grabbed the bucket from her and poured the water back into the lake. She could feel pure rage in his actions, his strong arm, his hard set face. His anger was directed at her.

He had pushed her down with so much force, Cara found she could not move straight away. A listlessness had descended on her too. She didn't have the will or the energy to attempt movement. She lay there, the commotion continuing in the background. Then she heard a scream.

She lifted her head and saw the flames of the hut flicker in the wind and bend towards the lake. The flame had barely touched the surface when there was a huge explosion. As if the lake itself had exploded. Now the whole sky was on fire.

She realised with surprise that the lake was on fire. Cara watched amazed as those glorious red, orange, gold flames flickered and danced up from the surface of the lake. The fire and its flames fed by the lake's water. She was in such shock from the sight and so much physical pain from the villager's brutal handling of her, she could not move at first, not even enough to drag herself away from the lake to safety. The villagers were running in all directions, the controlled feeling of panic had now gone mad. Panic was all around, on the surface, visible and palpable. Some villagers were shouting, some screaming, some running with confusion and fear written all over their faces. As she watched, Cara saw that they were grabbing what possessions they could in all that confusion and then running, eventually in the same direction, away from the lake and the village. She knew she had to do the same, but her mind wasn't working and her body refused to move.

She saw the little girl. The girl was alone. She looked dazed still and wasn't moving anywhere either, fixed like stone to her spot, rooted into the ground, with an uncomprehending terror staring out of her eyes. She was in imminent danger from the flames, raging in all directions fiercely, but no one came to her help.

The fear Cara felt in her heart for the girl's safety was way stronger than any she felt for her own life and it forced her into motion. She ran to the girl, grabbed her hand and started running away from the lake as the others were doing, following them as best she could. The girl was not easy to lead. Her steps were dragging, her movements slow and heavy, but Cara kept pulling. Danger gave her strength. She had no choice. She had to save the girl.

The heat of the flames was unbearable. She could hear the fire hissing, crackling, at times exploding. Each explosion like a dynamite ignited by one of the flames. She could not see anything around her. Her head hurt from the inside. Flammable water, that must be it, the answer. And she had drunk some. She had felt dizzy, confused and nauseous since. Was it some kind of drug in the water that made the villagers dazed and mechanic, unseeing in this world, unaware of their surroundings?

She understood the warning she had felt in her heart, but did not regret staying. At least now she knew... As long as she could save the girl all would be okay in the end.

She ran on, dragging the girl with her, half carrying her fragile, light body, half dragging her along the sand. In spite of all her effort and what seemed to her like an eternity of struggling with the girl, she could still feel the heat of the flames on her shoulders. She had gained hardly any distance between herself and the furious fire. Her strength was diminishing. She could feel it drain out of her. It was hard work pulling the girl along with her. Light as the girl was, she wasn't moving her legs at all, Cara was having to drag her dead weight through the sand, the friction making her onward movement even harder. Not being able to make any head way was distressing Cara and the heat and hissing of the flames were draining her will. She wanted to give up, lie down and watch as the flames devoured all in its path. But she kept going. She became aware once more of that instinctive drive in humans to stay alive at all costs. A drive that overrode physical weakness and mental resistance, giving the person more strength and will than they seemingly possessed. The desire to live had a drive of its own that was far greater than any resistance body and mind could offer. Cara caved into this animal instinct and let it take over her.

She saw a cave like feature appear a little ahead of them. She could hear human sounds coming out of it. She threw everything she had left in her into taking those last few steps. She pushed the girl through the entrance and followed her in, falling to her knees as she arrived.

A silence descended on the gathering as soon as she found herself on her knees in the cave, with the villagers looking down on her and the girl. The girl had fallen into a heap just ahead of her. Someone pushed her into a corner, where the girl lay completely still, her back turned to the rest of them, so still she might have been dead. Her body looked so lifeless, Cara wondered for a moment whether she had dragged a dead body all that distance. That certainly would have explained the unexpected weight and lack of movement or fear in the girl. The girl had lost any interest in staying alive. Was she even aware of what life was? Whether her efforts for the girl had been pointless or not, Cara knew that trying to save that little girl's life was the only thing that had saved her own life, so in some weird, indirect way she knew there had been a point to it, even if the girl had not made it.

The gathering was staring down at her. No one walked over to the girl to see if she was okay. There was no sign of welcome, gratitude or relief in their faces. There was no surprise either. Cara was too tired to try to communicate or understand. She was too dazzled and drained to make any further effort. She remained collapsed on the spot and closed her eyes.

She could hear the people around her talking in low tones with gruff, throaty voices. She could not understand a word of what they were saying, but judging by the closeness and direction of the voices she could tell they were standing around her. "They must be talking about me" she thought. She decided to let fate have its way and chose to keep her eyes closed, waiting for their decision.

She must have fallen asleep while they were still talking. She woke up in darkness and quiet. Inside the cave was pitch black and she could not tell whether she was alone or not at first. She soon realised she was not alone from the sound of breathing a little to her left. The entrance to the cave must have been shut, for there was not even a tiny stray bit of light coming from anywhere, nor a breeze or wisp of air. She had a sudden desire to run away. "A bit late now" she thought to herself sarcastically, for the first time annoyed that she had not heeded her warning instincts. She had no idea which way the entrance was any longer. And even if she found it, she wasn't convinced she'd be able to open it without waking the others. Their bizarre attitude and behaviour forbade her to do anything that might annoy or upset them. Anyway, they had let her stay with them, so they obviously meant no harm. Still, she felt unsure. She could not tell what they were about and wondered what they meant to do with her in the morning. She felt like a prisoner, locked up in some unknown corner of the world, surrounded by strangers, with an air of danger hanging around them.

She lay awake the rest of the night, thinking over what she

had seen of them and their ways. The mystery of the lake had been solved, but what about the rest?

She thought of how dizzy she had felt after drinking from the lake and how the world around her had become vague. She hadn't cared what would happen to her. She had been so indifferent, it was as if she had been under the spell of a drug. Tenzin had told her about some herbs that led the users to lose connection with their surroundings. She had told her that it was a way of escaping this world and all feeling. "It numbs the head and the heart" she had said, "That might be welcome at times, but it also leads to ignorance. It is always better to understand, know and feel, even when it brings suffering, rather than avoid all feeling in unconscious bliss".

The day she had been thrown back into her own village, abandoned and hurt, she would have given anything for some of those herbs, but she understood now why feeling was better than not feeling and she was glad none had been available. The stony, blank eyes of the villagers had scared her. They were so cut off from reality and even from their own existence. She would not want to be like that. Better feel her heart, even if what she felt was daggers and pain. Her heart could also love, cherish and be grateful. These people were dead to themselves. What was the point of being alive, if there was no life?

She wondered if this drug also caused rage and anger. Some herbs did when their effect wore off. Was the villagers' source now dried out with the burning of the lake? How would they respond to that? And what about the lake? Surely all that water could not burn? Maybe it would be drinkable now. Maybe the drug element of it had burned off in the fire.

She wished she could see the stars for some comfort and guidance, but she had to settle into the darkness. She was probably safe till day break anyway.

She was not able to really settle or calm herself, even though she tried. The night passed slowly. It felt like years had gone by when she heard the first stirrings somewhere in the cave. She wondered how big it was, the sounds were not close.

Even after people started waking up and communicating, it felt like a long wait to Cara before anything happened. They were obviously in no hurry to move and no one left their place for a while.

Eventually someone did start to move. She guessed he or she was crawling from the shuffling sounds she could hear. There was a bang, a scraping noise and then she saw light flooding into the cave through a long crack. The crack grew wider, the whole cave gradually becoming bright with sunlight. For a few moments she was blinded by the intensity of the light. When her eyes started to see again, at first all she saw was an empty space in front of her.

She was in a hollow space, the sand around her was hard, like stone. It was clean and bare. She saw the man who had crawled over to open the entrance. He was sitting back on his heels, staring out into the desert. She had to turn all the way around and look behind her to see the rest of them. They were all lying or sitting, huddled together in a corner. They were as far away as they physically could be from her, as if she had the potential to spread poison from her body. Seeing them, her body was overcome by weariness once more. A heaviness descended on her and she wished for the safety and stillness of the previous darkness she had so wholly wished to see the last of only moments ago.

The villagers took a long time to get up. Every movement of theirs was slow, forced out of their body with intense deliberation and effort. Cara watched mesmerised. They moved as if they were made of rusty metal or cold, hard stone. They moved like lifeless objects, their souls had left them long ago.

Slowly and gradually they all managed to drag themselves up and they moved to the entrance one at a time, each person taking ages and no one in a hurry to get out. Each one of them, as soon as they reached the end of the cave and beginning of the outer world, gazed out into the distance for a while before taking their first step into the desert. Not a single one of them as much as glanced in her direction. When the last one had left, Cara got up too. She had been waiting impatiently, both hoping and dreading that one of them would speak to her, or do something, at least acknowledge her existence in some way. But none did.

She walked out into the bright sunshine and heat. She wanted to see what had happened to the lake and the village and what the villagers were going to do about it. Just as she was about to follow them, something made her stop and look back. She noticed that the little girl she had brought there the night before was still lying in the exact same spot as she had been pushed into when they had arrived.

Cara was afraid of what she might find out, what she already knew in her heart, but was unwilling to recognise as yet. But her body would not allow her to leave the girl lying there alone, so she walked over to her. The girl hadn't moved at all. Her eyes stared out straight ahead of her, but they were blank and unseeing. There was no movement anywhere in her face or body. Cara crouched down next to her and neared her ear to the girl's nostrils. She detected no breath. She held the girls freezing cold wrist for minutes, without any sign of a pulse. She could feel panic rising in her. It was near the surface, but Cara knew she could not succumb. It would do no one any good and she was afraid that if even a little part of that panic surfaced, Cara would be taken over by it, left ineffective, unable to think or move. She wanted to leave. She was dying to leave. She controlled her fear and pushed the panic back down her throat and locked it up in her chest, forcefully controlling her breath and ordering her heart to slow down.

She felt anger rise up in her. She hated these people, so cold and unfeeling, lacking any compassion or care. She hated the people who could leave a little girl in the corner of a dark damp cave, leaving her to death and her dead body to rot or be torn apart by insects and animals. She hated them all and her hatred spread out to the desert. She hated this place. Anger, hatred, rage rising in her, tears filling her eyes, she sighed, a croaky, forceful sigh. She dropped the girl's limp wrist, her anger turning to pain and compassion. She felt sorry for the girl, who had never stood a chance, born into this God forsaken village, amongst these cold, uncaring people. She never had a chance. Her rage turned to God, "why? Why? Why? It's unfair" she screamed. Her tears started flowing down her cheeks. She was gasping for breath, the anger in her chocking her throat.

She cried for a while, letting emotions flow out of her through her tears. Gradually they lessened in intensity. Tiredness started to take over her body. She knew she had to leave. She lifted herself up from the crumpled position she now found herself in. She looked back at the girl and gently closed her eyelids over her blind, staring eyes, leaving her in complete inner darkness. She kissed the girls forehead and prayed she might find ease, spirit and life wherever her journey took her next. "I hope your next life will be a better one" she thought. She prayed that things would be easier for her there. She deserved it considering the short life she had led in this odd world. She covered the girl with her own shawl and feeling more tired than ever, walked out of the hut.

She could see the gathering of huts in the distance. The scars left by the fire were visible even from that distance. Some huts were in ruins, most charred to black. There were burnt ashes and charred material scattered all over. The place looked and smelled of devastation. The only sight unchanged was that of the lake, its water shining brightly in the sunlight, beckoning to those who felt tired, hot and thirsty. The contrast was striking; the glorious, unspoilt, pure beauty of the water and the utter devastation this seeming beauty had brought to its surroundings. Cara was once more filled with awe. The beauty and shining purity of the lake made her question her own sanity. How could this seemingly glorious source of life, shining and sparkling possibly have caused death and destruction.

Cara shook herself. She had had enough. She did not want

to see any more. She did not care about these people. Her hatred towards them lingered on in her. She felt sick to her stomach with the indifference they had shown, their lack of consciousness, their cold, blank, unseeing stares and dead, unfeeling hearts. Their careless treatment of their own child was shocking. The sight of that poor little dead girl haunted her. She wanted no more from this place. She walked away slowly in the opposite direction with a heavy heart and weary limbs.

She continued her journey through the golden desert, day after day, week after week. As with every other experience and intense emotion of her life, the memories and feelings from the poisonous lake and its living ghosts faded from her heart and mind over time. The girl haunted her with lessening intensity and her rage and sorrow subsided.

Her days took on a monotonous quality, each similar, one to the other. The occasional appearance of a cluster of huts or tents, the essential sources of water, wells and lakes, the vegetation she came across that provided her with nourishment, they all blended into each other, parts of a large puzzle, different shades of a large mosaic. People she came across and interacted with blended in with their surroundings, none standing out, none remaining in her memory for long. She settled back into a comfortable routine of walking, seeing, watching, letting thoughts and feelings flow through her, paying attention to them, but being careful not to get stuck on any one for too long. If a thought or emotion persisted, she consciously put it away from her mind. She had learned that going deeper and deeper into one thought or feeling only led to circular thinking, looping round endlessly, creating frustration, without reaching clarity, understanding or any resolution. The only way to put something to rest with understanding was to let it go for a while, until it returned to her with its accompanying answer or solution. She allowed herself to be led, rather than forcing herself in any one direction. She succumbed to the greater wisdom of nature and the universe, allowing herself to become small and pliant. She realised that this was her current route to inner peace. Letting go, not willing an end, but following the path set before her.

The days followed one after the other, weeks and months passed by. Cara was feeling her heart soften and her body lighten. She gradually stopped struggling for answers. All she needed to do was keep walking. The answers came when the time was right. Another dream had been visiting her recently, bringing calm and faith to her troubled heart. With each appearance of this dream, Cara felt herself a little more renewed, more confident and at peace with herself, her circumstances and the world in general.

She had been dreaming of the tree of life. It had a welcoming air about it. It grew out of a large rock, just big enough to hold the tree's vast roots. The rock stood isolated in the middle of a lake. The tree's thick trunk was gnarly. At the top, branches sprouted out in all directions like an umbrella. The branches were covered in leaves. The tree spoke to her of wisdom. It offered a refuge under its wide, strong, thick, green branches. It was a solitary island, yet it did not feel lonely. It was interlinked with its surroundings, the rock and the sea. It was connected to nature, to humans and to the whole universe. It was part of a whole and whole within itself. It communicated serenity and peace. It spoke of the joy of life and the strength to stand alone, tall and proud. It had its own individual base out of which its roots flourished and through which it was nourished. Her tree was beautiful, solid, free, proud and strong. It smiled at her with warmth. Its branches welcomed her like the arms of a lover. Its leaves were vibrant with life and they whispered musically in the wind. Cara wanted to stay in its cool shade, amongst its welcoming smells forever.

After waking up, every time she had seen the tree of life in her dream, Cara felt better within herself, happier, more whole, more at peace and more serene. Her body felt renewed and vibrant, her soul bigger, her feelings more grounded, her mind clearer. She welcomed the day, excited and hopeful of what it might bring. She felt a renewed sense of interest and aliveness awakening within her day by day, dream by dream.

Her tree rooted deep into the solid, nurturing ground

and grew out of it with strong trunk and branches, reaching up to the bright blue sky. It connected earth and heaven, feminine and masculine, yin and yang. It spoke of wholeness of opposites through acceptance. Not preferring one or the other, but taking from both, combining them within itself and spreading out from that place of completeness and inclusion.

Its message to her was the need for her to connect her small, pained soul with the greater oneness of the universe, thereby taking on its limitless, endless potential. Finding within herself, not by denying or ignoring, but by seeing, understanding and accepting, a connection to God, to the whole of the universe, with all its conflicts and turmoil, with its nights and days, its dark and light, its seen and recognised and its denied and ignored.

She knew the tree mirrored her and her ultimate goal. Each man and woman was already whole within themselves, if only they could see that, recognise it and let go of their struggle against their individual attributes and their denial of elements they feared. If everyone could love and forgive all the bad as well as the good, if they could take it all in, bringing shadow to light and breath of life to death, they would grow strong and be at peace within themselves.

She felt that the answer to all her questions, the peace, serenity, joy, love and connection to God she searched for, all already existed within her, if she could let her roots spread deep into the earth and reach her branches high up into the sky, feeling and learning from the feminine, reaching towards and connecting to the masculine. Her growth would come from the earth and her will from the sky. Without the earth she would die. She was alone, yet once connected to her inner soul, she would be one with the universe, able to take it all in, and love it completely.

Her heart gladdened by these dreams. There was hope and joy yet for her. She wanted to put her arms around the trunk of a real tree, feeling its strength, solidity, wisdom and energy, but there were no trees in the desert and part of her did not expect to ever see one again. So she brought the image of her dreams to her mind whenever she felt her heart sinking, her soul questioning or her spirit darkening. It helped, every time...

She found herself becoming ever more peaceful, walking through the now familiar terrain, her mind empty at times, at times listening, at times dreaming. Sometimes memories took over and then she would exert herself to push them away. Sometimes if she felt desolate, she prayed or she imagined herself under the tree of life, feeling its wholesome energy seep into her, spreading into her every cell, nourishing, revitalising, filling her. She felt herself gradually become a part of the tree, one with it. And her soul gladdened and peace blossomed within her.

Sometimes she questioned her whole journey. What was the point? Why bother? But whenever she thought "why bother", her answer was always "what alternative do I have?" Staying still meant death and pain. As long as she kept moving she could keep her memories away from the surface, away from her heart. The effort to walk and survive replaced desolation and despair, taking first place in her being, while what was painful retreated into the background. But the dark thoughts were always alert, at the ready, waiting for a quiet moment, one when she was off her guard and her immediate surroundings and needs had moved back from her surface consciousness. Then they would throw themselves at her with full force, taking over her whole being until she felt tired and defeated. Each time she had to go back into battle with them and fight them until they retreated and allowed her heart to have some space to beat.

Dark and negative thoughts did not help her, but with prayers and images and most importantly by not surrendering to defeat and constantly moving on, continuing with her journey, she managed to keep them back just enough to survive. She knew their strength decreased day by day. She realised that they only crept up once in a while now and it required much less effort to defeat them than it had done before. Even for this small miracle Cara felt gratitude towards the universe. It had given her heart ache, loss and struggles, but it had also given her guidance, teachers and the desert. She knew her painful memories and the heartache they carried with them would leave her eventually. If not completely, at least enough for her to live again.

The poppy

One night, as she settled herself to rest, she felt a change in the wind. There was a different taste to it, a freshness, a new smell. "A new phase of my journey is about to begin" she thought. She felt ready to leave the desert and enter this new phase that was waiting for her. She was curious and mildly excited.

The next morning, after about an hour of walking, the wind feeling fresher on her face than it had done, a gentle breeze rustling her hair, she came upon a bright red flower, growing tall and upright in the middle of the sand. It was the only growing plant around. The red of the flower was vivid and vibrant. It looked so fragile there in the middle of harsh heat and sand, yet it stood erect and proud, undaunted by its surroundings.

Cara was amazed at its courage and strength, its ability to hold its own against its harsh surroundings. It stood contrary to nature, yet also a part it. She felt overwhelmed by the beauty of the flower. Two leaves grew out of its stem, both vibrant green. The flower reminded Cara of herself. She too was standing alone in harsh surroundings. She too must have held a strength worthy of respect to survive her journey so far. And yet Cara knew she was fragile inside. She had managed to survive the desert, the fire, heartbreak and months of walking in overwhelming heat. She had been hungry and thirsty, she had felt fatigue and helplessness. She had held her head up proud in front of any living creature, standing her ground, believing in her journey and the honesty and truth of her actions. Yet she could have been killed or broken so easily at any time.

The vibrant, red of the flower created a stark contrast to its ever same, greyish yellow surroundings. The heat creating a dry mist close to the earth and the flower shining through the mist, a centre of energy and life. Cara wanted so much to take the flower and carry it with her as a reminder of beauty, vibrancy and life, vulnerability and strength, but she could not bear to be the cause of its death. Instead she sat down facing it and watched it gently move in the breeze. She imprinted the image in her heart, every detail, every shade and line.

As she watched, she sensed the flower's message. She thought of strict ideals, separation between good and bad, right and wrong, light and dark. How she had always strived to be good, right and light, shunning the shadow elements of her being, trying to better them, change them, get rid of them. How the people around her had always judged her, each other and themselves, driven by a desperate need to hold on to strict rules. All that was deemed not good and not light was shunned and punished. Yet this glorious flower held it all within its one fragile body with pride. It said "Look, I'm fragile, but I am proud of my thin stem and dainty petals, my strength lies in my knowledge and acceptance of all that I am, as I am and my acceptance of myself gives me the strength to survive and the striking beauty you are now marvelling at".

The flower's red was the colour of live giving blood. It was defiant against any hardship the world could send its way. It swayed in such a gentle, soft manner, Cara felt that it was able to accept nature and be part of it and flow with it naturally. It was not rigid or angry, it had not grown stiff through its defiance. Its defiance held within it an understanding of nature, an ability to bend to nature's wills, a softness of attitude, a pliancy that held strength in its flexibility.

She felt freedom in the flower, freedom in its knowledge that it had a right to be there. And strength in understanding its place in the world, accepting it and growing from it and through it.

As Cara looked on, she felt a surge of anger rise in her chest. So much had been taken from her in her early life, so much denied. Her very existence and being had been denied by her mother. Her right to be, live and be happy had been denied her. She had had to squash her own vibrant spirit. She had had to struggle for her right to exist, for her right to live her own truth, fighting every step of the way.

She allowed the urge to fight and struggle ease away from her body, feeling her chest and arms soften in the process. Gratitude replaced anger in her heart, gratitude towards the beauty of the flower, gratitude that it existed and that it had shared its spirit with her. Gratitude that she had survived and that God had given her this day of life, which had brought her to this vision of immense beauty.

Cara was amazed at the shift that occurred within her as she watched. She felt the warm glow of gratitude in her body, the fiery red vibrancy, the tall, slender, proud beauty, and yet at the same time she felt the burning anger, the resentment and sadness. What amazed her was that she could hold these conflicting sensations within herself simultaneously, without having to force either one away, without shirking from either of them, accepting and holding these opposites simultaneously, together.

"This is what the flower is teaching me", she thought, "how to hold light and shadow together, strength and fragility, courage and humility, how to accept them all as a part of me, and learn to love the holder of this wide spectrum of emotions, with all its conflicting, opposite variations".

A sense of confidence spread through her, she felt her body lengthen, her face smile. Her wish had been granted. She had the flower with her now and would always carry it with her as part of her being. The flower was an image of herself and Cara felt happy with the flower that was within her and happy with herself, who was the flower.

Nothing to obstruct their light
In that split second of their choosing
Life is illuminated, inner soul blooming.
And sight is offered in all clarity

What a wonder life can be
The energy flows from within each being
And seated in the centre, yet swimming free
The cool water flowing past
Seagulls shrieking, one with the breeze
A pearl glitters as life floats past
Reach out, but don't steal the jewel
It belongs there, in the depths of the ocean
It's beauty joyful for all to see
But burden and sorrow it would bring
To him who tried to own it selfishly

Cara had never seen the ocean. She hadn't even ever seen a drawing of it. She had heard it talked about though. There were many stories and myths about the ocean and the otherworldly creatures that came out of its depths. She had heard the ocean described sometimes as a powerful monster, all devouring, loud and awesome. Sometimes it was a giver of life, energising, awakening, free flowing. She had heard tales in which incredible creatures came out of its depths to bring death and destruction on people. And yet sometimes it produced maidens and mermaids that guided the weary, lost traveller.

The roar against the shores had been described to her by those who had heard it. She had been told of the speed with which it rushed in and out of land, racing with itself, tumbling over its own steps, falling over, picking itself up and continuing on, pushing down water ahead of it to rise up above itself, only to be pushed back down by a wave speeding up behind it once again. A never ending chase, each wave roaring with anger, energy and excitement.

She had heard of the mouth of the sea, taller than the tallest tree, threatening, ready to devour anything that came within its reach. A mouth that could swallow anything in its path whole, no matter how big. But for all the stories and descriptions she had heard, she had never been able to visualise it properly. When she dreamt of the sea it was as a dark grey monster, with no arms and many huge mouths, angry and fierce. It came to her vision as a hectic, confused creature, angry, impatient and demonic.

She could not have said what she expected to see if she ever reached the ocean. She had never expected to see it in person. When she had thought about it, she had wondered if she would be taken over with awe and terror. But then she remembered other, conflicting stories too that told of a different creature. Ones that told of a gentle, vast lake of water, smooth and blue, cool and comforting with beautiful mermaids playing in its arms.

She could not combine the monster with the mermaid. Maybe the ocean was like a confused man, humble and hard working during the day, sociable towards friends and acquaintances, until he had had a few drinks, after which he would return home a monster, shouting at and beating his wife and children. Perhaps it was a being with many characters and no one could tell which of its many characters it would don when the sun rose to start a new day.

Or maybe there were many different oceans, all with their own personality traits, taking turns to appear at the shores, while the other characters took rest. Maybe just as there were different kinds of people, some kind, some evil, some a mixture of good and bad, some giving, some taking, some healing, some killing, so it was with vast waters, an interchangable community of different beings.

To her it seemed, the ocean must be a god with human characteristics. Able to devour humans, ships and anything else that humans were capable of building, able to control and destroy nature and yet when it chose to, able to give comfort, support and life.

She realised as soon as she caught sight of the ocean, that nothing she had heard about it could have ever prepared her for the actual experience of reaching it.

First she heard it, before she had seen even a glimpse of it in the distance. The sky was covered in dark, heavy clouds. They hung low, grey and pregnant with life giving water. She knew rain was imminent. How she desired to feel rain drops on her face and body. She had been dry for too long. She felt she could not have too much water in any form. Though the clouds looked menacing, her heart welcomed them. Her body welcomed the thought of feeling wet and cool. Her lips yearned for drops of rain on them and water flowing through her lips into her parched throat and burning insides.

The sound had started as a distant murmur at first. A wail in deep notes. She could not place it. She was not expecting the ocean. She wondered if the gods were mourning, if someone had lost a loved one. Her heart grew heavy and dark like the clouds, remembering those she had lost forever. How was her little boy? What was he doing now? She knew the rider would take good care of him, but how could a boy learn gentleness and compassion without the loving presence of his mother. He would grow to be harsh and cruel like the rest of them. She felt a surge of resentment and bitter anger. It was her right to bring her own son up. How dare they rob her of this natural, universally accepted right?

And what if he got sick. Who would nurse him? Sickness. She was suddenly reminded that in that harsh environment they had surrounded themselves with, the riders had no time, patience or compassion for the sick. She herself felt sick, as concern spread in the pit of her stomach. If either her baby boy, or her still, in spite of everything, loved rider should get ill or wounded, they would be left to die unless healing was going to be easy and they would not be a burden to others while they got better. "I would have taken care of them" she thought.

She sat down, surrounded by the wailing sound coming from the distance. It was an expression of her own feelings and she felt the need to be with it for a while. She let the sound take over her whole body and felt her body pulsate to its rhythm.

She tried to remember what she had learned from Tenzin so long ago. "Don't fight it" Tenzin used to say. "Nature has its own laws and man and woman must obey them. Nature will always have its own way. We either flow with it, or die fighting it. If we choose to fight it, we are choosing a battle we cannot win". Tenzin had taught her to love the ways of nature, but it was different then. She was different then. She had felt so full of love and life, she could have loved anyone and accepted anything. Nobody was outside of the scope of her compassion and care.

Now she felt no love at all. She had lost interest in the ways of nature. She had not read the stars for a long time. She had lost confidence in their guidance. She had lost her trust in the ways of the universe. How could it be so cruel? And why should she love that which created so much pain and suffering?

Somehow the rhythm of the ocean moving her body started to gradually calm her. She felt a gentleness take over. She heard the wailing sound like a beckoning now, an invitation to the unknown. She thought "the gods are mourning with me. My heart is beating to their rhythm. They hear me, they understand and they are supporting me through it. What I feel is right and this is where I belong at the moment".

She sat for a while longer, feeling strength and will return to her heart and limbs. Until gradually she felt ready to move on. There was no point staying still for much longer. She must continue and find the loud wailer that had helped her crushed, buried mourning surface and that had kept her company through her grief, mourning with her.

She got up slowly. She felt tired and heavy. She started walking forwards, towards the sound. The air was getting heavier by the minute, as if there were buckets full of water hanging in it. She wondered if the water particles in the air would explode, they felt so dense. She felt her body mirror the sensation, feeling heavy all over.

As she walked slowly on, the sound grew louder. It became more like a roar. She was getting close. A wild energy was rising into the air and spreading outwards from somewhere in the distance. Whatever the source of this energy was, must be strong, stronger than anything she had ever seen before. But it did not feel menacing. It simply was. "Acceptance" she thought.

A few more steps and she was over a mound of sand. Suddenly she was there, facing the unknown and indescribable.

She stopped in her tracks. Her eyes grew wide. The sight was beyond anything she had ever imagined. To her eyes, the vision was other-worldly, incredible. The energy of the place, the noise, the vast expanse of pure wild movement, the rush, the strength, she had no words that could give what she saw and felt justice.

She felt fully alive, the ocean roaring within her very body and soul. She wanted to breathe it all in, the heavy air, · the roaring sound, the dense energy, the wild strength. She desired to make the experience a part of her, so she could carry it with her. She felt a tremor of expectation shiver up her body. She felt impatient. She could not wait to touch it, feel it, get to know it. She felt restless with anticipation. She felt excited in a way she hadn't felt for many years, not since she was a little girl when life had still held the power to excite her. She had thought that potential had passed away long ago, yet here she was, feeling excited, joyful even. She had an immense desire to become one with this almighty source of energy, power and life. "The gods are passing on their energy to me" she thought, gratefully. She yearned for joy and the feeling of being full of life. She grasped her excitement. Something in her soul that she had thought dead and buried was now calling out to her and she didn't want to let it go. She didn't dare soften her grasp. She remembered how in the past everything new had held excitement for her and she felt that feeling of anticipation return. She held on to it like a long lost friend, left for dead, but returned after many years of absence.

She hurried on towards the sound. A picture arose in her mind. She imagined strong arms enveloping her fragile little body, the wail rising up from its chest and seeping through its embrace in to her poor worn out bones.

Before she knew it she was staring the monster in the face, close up. Its hissing, roaring spitting wetting her face, the taste of salt on her lips.

No, what she saw was nothing she could have expected. It was beyond any description, any work of imagination. It was too vast and alive to be captured in words. So much energy emanated out of it, no story could hold it, no painting contain it. The sound it made was louder than any pack of animals she had ever heard. Even gods could not compete with this vast, limitless creature, singing, shouting, roaring, rushing in and out. All powerful, overwhelming in its awesome strength and size and beautiful, glorious and yet playful. She could not take it all in, not at once.

Even the colour was beyond anything she had ever seen before. So much depth to it, so many different shades, the colours changing as she watched, a grey blue green mixture, blending, transforming, both absorbing and reflecting light at the same time. "No wonder I've never seen a picture of it" she thought. How could anyone paint life and energy itself?"

She saw its mouths. Jaws without teeth, taller and bigger than giants. They could easily eat up a whole village. But the mouths weren't still, they opened and shut foaming white as they closed in. There were so many of them, countless, hungry, foaming mouths. Huge caverns opening, screaming and roaring, smashing shut only for other mouths to open. They were everywhere and nowhere at the same time. A constantly moving, changing vision right there before her eyes.

She stood rooted to her spot, gazing out in awe. She felt a surge of energy in her body and a sense of deep peace and contentment holding the energy close in her ribs. "I will never leave these shores" she thought, "Life has been worth living just for this one moment. My life culminates in this one glorious moment. To my suffering I am grateful, as it has led me to this experience. This sense of connection, peace with everything in the universe, peace with myself and a sense of belonging in the world, oneness with this vast monster. The unending, limitless sea, it must be God itself and it is calling to me, embracing me from outside and calling upon me from inside my very own body. Life, love, power, anger, rage, the universe and little me, all combining into this one vast source of energy".

She felt the flow of water, the cleansing, stirring effect of the ocean reach within her body, cleansing away her pain and turmoil, settling her worries and screams, bringing peace into her troubled heart. A deep serenity growing, growing in her heart and in her chest. "I love you", she whispered, "I love you. Thank you".

She walked out on to the sand, feeling the soft give of the ground, allowing her feet to sink in before taking the next step, enjoying the gentle yield and the grounding stability of the sand under and around her feet. She sat down gently, slowly, not taking her eyes away from the ocean for a second. She sat still watching her new friend, her new mentor and teacher. Eventually fatigue took over her and she lay down. She closed her eyes, letting the voice of the ocean move within her. She felt calm and happy, at peace with herself and the world, safe, comforted, supported and taken care of. She drifted out of consciousness.

Just as she had known a few years ago, that she had to leave her home, even though she didn't know where she was going, other than it had to be far away, she knew once more what she needed to do. She could not imagine where her path would now lead her and once again she had no idea if she would survive, although over time she had grown stronger and more confident. She felt wiser too. She was content with her place in the world and had faith in the path that the universe kept stretching out in front of her, into the unknown, ever changing in form, surroundings and experiences.

She felt she would make it through to the other side and was excited, with a sense of adventure throbbing in her veins. God had guided her well so far. She had been sure she would die before, she had even wanted death, hoped for it, with all her heart, and yet she had survived. Her soul had wanted to never wake up, to not have to go on, to cease existing, and yet a deeper energy, a deeper will and a shove from the universe had kept her going. She had travelled far and come far with strength and confidence growing in her heart. She knew within her mind and soul that she would survive the next phase of her journey as well. She felt no concern or fear.

She also knew that if she didn't survive, she would only have perished if that was what was meant to be. If now was her time, so be it. She had no desire to cling on to life without consciousness, doggedly, unnecessarily, once it was time to move away from it. She did not want to find an escape away from God's plan for her. All she was sure of was that she needed to follow her heart and read and hear the signs the universe sent her. As long as she followed her intuition, her conscience would be clear and she could move forward with confident, calm steps.

She knew she needed to enter the ocean, to become one with it. She was drawn into its energy, wanting to dive into the depths of this source of life. She wanted to feel the ocean in all its glory and power. It was a monster she intrinsically trusted. It beckoned her.

She took her first few steps into the ocean timidly. She felt the cool strong caress of the water as she allowed her body to move into it, gradually and gently sinking into its hold. The sound the ocean made had turned into a deep-throated vibration, giving life to her body through direct contact. Her skin felt soft and beautiful in the water. The coolness of its caress revived her tired spirit.

As she sank deeper she started to move her arms, uncertainly at first, gently, feeling the soft but strong resistance of the water surrounding her. Then she started to swim, her arms feeling stronger with each stroke. Pushing against the water to propel herself forward. The water both slowing her down, barring her way subtly and at the same time becoming the force against which she could move forward. It gave way at times, drawing her below its surface, preventing air from entering her lungs, then thrusting her back up for breath.

What was at first uncertain, insecure movements, turned into rhythmic, calm strokes. The rhythm taking over her soul, a deep meditative quality enveloping her being, peace surrounding her heart and calm soaking into her mind.

Once, as the waves pushed her back down underneath their surface, she was struck by an odd thought "it's pitch black down here, there's not even a glimmer of light, yet I can see perfectly. How is that possible?" She saw no source of light, no reflection or glitter on the ground or rocks, yet she could see the deep darkness ahead and the shadows within it. She wanted to move into that darkness. There was something comforting and constant about it. She drew a deep breath and dived.

As alien and new as this space was for her, she still felt calm inside, deeply serene, comforted and protected. "I feel safe, for the first time in my life, I feel truly safe. I'm under water, in pitch black darkness, in the unknown, yet I feel safe. How can it be?". She thought of the monster stories and the tales she had heard describing the creatures that were meant to live in deep dark waters. Yet still she did not feel afraid.

She felt the power of the ocean, the power of the universe, the strength of God. But they weren't asserting themselves from the outside. She felt them contained within her own body. The roaring of the water, the soothing yet powerful energy of the ocean surrounding her, holding her, holding the source of the universe within her. "Only something as powerful and vast as the ocean could ever contain my spirit" she thought, "it is right I should move in it, with it and be destroyed by it if that is its plan" The whole universe contained in this vast ocean and the universe and ocean contained within her. She felt infinite and glorious, beautiful and free, full of life and joy, calm and happy. She felt God's love and support, her faith awake within her, speaking to her through the existence of this substance, moving and alive. She felt all emotions, all source of life within her body overflowing out of her heart.

She felt a sense of joy rise up from her chest in to her throat, spreading to her cheeks and eyes. She knew she was smiling and that tears were flowing down her cheeks at the same time. "I'm happy to be here", she thought. "I'm grateful".

Her arms were finding their strength, stroke after stroke. The deeper she swam, the stronger she grew. She knew the only direction she could go in was down. Moving up, going back were simply not options. She felt the urge to continue downward, further into the depths. Her joy kept rising, propelling her on faster and faster. She felt no fear at all. Stronger arms, broader strokes, darker, cooler water, further and further down, deeper into safety, deeper into the pit of the ocean.

She thought of him, on his horse, as he turned round and left, taking her boy with him, taking her love, her heart, her joy and hope away on his tall horse, away where she could no longer reach them, never again hold them. Her heart wrenched for a moment. Was it for him, or their son, or both, or neither? "Don't think about that now, stay with the water" she thought. She felt the cool, fluid embrace around her arms and hands. She felt the flowing, ever-changing energy of the water seep through her fingertips, up her arms and down her whole body.

The water soothed, it cleansed, it flowed drawing out stuck stagnation from within her. Breaking up the stillness, warming the cold, soothing the knots and aches. The water washed away the poison that had been cruising round her veins for the past few years; the poison of loss and pain, of heartbreak and regret. For this moment, at this moment, for now, there was no pain or loss, she held neither heartbreak, nor memories of the past. All she felt was peace and calm, joy and a feeling of gratitude. "stay with it, stay with the flow" she thought, "such a welcome break from life and hardship, stay with it."

As she continued on, she noticed something in the quality of the water shift and change. She caught the slightest glimmer of it, it was still too far away to see fully, beyond the reach of her eye. It was gone in a second or two, but she noticed a flicker, as if light played with water molecules somewhere far ahead. She wondered where it could have possibly come from. She was so deep now, no light could penetrate down into these layers, they were meant to exist in darkness, darkness became this place on earth. And even if light could penetrate this far, she would have seen it break the darkness from above, cutting through layers of water, reflecting back, spreading out. But the speck of light she had seen for a split moment had come from a different source, not from the surface, but from directly ahead of her, from deeper below, further down in the ocean. The memory of the light beckoned her.

She moved towards it, feeling excitement in her chest and arms. She wanted to see it, find it and learn from it, learn from its source, a creator of light other than the sun. She was curious and excited. She felt strong and intrigued. She felt interested. Her mind was racing with excitement and anticipation. There was no longer any sign of the light she had seen, but she knew it had not been her imagination. It was as real as the water surrounding her. She needed to find it and follow it to its source.

She was searching with her eyes for another glimmer, another sign. She strained her eyes, forcing sight, trying to see all around her, but she could see nothing light, nothing sparkled at her through the distance. She had nothing but an image to follow, the trail of a memory, one that could be wrong or misleading, the reality of which she was already questioning. She wasn't sure at all that she was swimming in the right direction. But it didn't matter. She had no other purpose, aim or direction anyway. It didn't matter which way she went, how far she swam. It didn't matter at all. The light had given her some kind of vague purpose. She needed a purpose. She grabbed this sign, this invitation, however fleeting it had been. She needed its guidance and the image of the light in her mind was strong enough to follow. She trusted her heart, her arms and the ocean and continued swimming, searching for her light.

The trap

She caught sight of the light once more. It was brighter now, she had swam nearer to its source. She dived down to try to reach the light. It shone upwards from the earth, glittering a dazzling bright, golden colour. It was shaped like a bangle.

Cara tried to reach it, but it kept evading her. She was grabbing handfuls of earth, but the bangle remained where it was, untouched, shining.

Cara closed her eyes and reached for the bangle without using sight. She stretched out her arm and there it was. She felt its warm surface against her fingers. It had a smooth surface and she grabbed it with ease. It felt as if the bangle had moved into her hand of its own accord, gliding through her fingers. She put her wrist through it and opened her eyes. The bangle was a perfect fit around her thin wrist. It was dazzlingly bright and beautiful. It felt comforting to have it wrapped close around her arm. She felt its vibrancy touching her skin, a pulsating sensation spreading out of the bangle and into her body as if it held its own current of energy, which it was pulsating into her body.

She continued to swim onwards, trusting the bangle would lead her where she needed to go. It had become her new guide, her star in this deep, lost world.

After a while Cara saw a shape emerge in front of her. As she neared the shape, its outline became clearer. Cara watched the shape of a woman gradually form before her eyes. She was wearing a long white dress. The dress was floating in the water, flowing gracefully around her body. A white veil, reached out towards the ground all around her. She was riding a white horse. Cara was struck by the woman's poise, both graceful and proud, yet keeping a sense of fragility about her, asking for compassion and help. Cara wondered if she'd ever seen a being so beautiful. At the same time she was aware of a sense of danger. The woman was cloaked with a cloud of threat and Cara's instincts were warning her, telling her she was being led into a trap, but Cara could not stop, the angelic beauty of the woman and her pure allure demanded she follow and Cara could not resist the temptation.

The white rider and her horse entered a structure made of white canvas and Cara followed them in with only a moment's hesitation. The sense of dread was growing in her chest. She found herself in a long corridor with rooms opening out in all directions as far as she could see. The woman continued riding straight on and Cara followed, until suddenly the rider turned to her right and entered through one of the openings. Cara's sense of impending danger grew too loud for her to ignore any longer. Her instincts were yelling at her to turn back and leave the white corridors, to turn away from the mystical rider. She wanted to obey, but her limbs continued moving her in the direction of the white rider. She entered through the opening in spite of her dread and her mind ordering her not to. The pull on her to follow had been too strong to disobey.

As soon as she stepped through the opening, she heard the entrance shut behind her. She knew she was trapped, she could doubt it no longer.

The room was foggy. There was light, but it was not from the sun or stars, it had an unnatural hazy quality to it, as if the room itself was the source of the misty, hazy light. The whole room was covered in grey, heavy mist. She could just about see, but her surroundings were vague and unclear. The room was neither light, nor dark, nor a shade in between the two. It was blurred and confused. She could feel the presence of others around her, but she could not see them. The air was getting denser and more oppressive with each breath, her breathing became shallower, restrained and increasingly effortful. The space felt small and constrained, although she could tell that

148

its dimensions were large. She could see no opening, no gap or crack in the canvas walls anywhere.

She walked back to where she had entered the room and touched the canvas, but the flowing, soft material turned to hard stone under her touch. She took her hand away and the canvas became soft and flowing once more. The canvas had a life of its own, the opening she had entered through magically disappearing in its folds and the canvas transforming from canvas to stone, and then back to canvas at will. She could not break through. As stone, it was hard, solid, unyielding. As canvas it tricked one to thinking it would yield easily, but it would not. Not to anyone who did not understand its nature. And Cara had no inkling what its mystery was or how to go about finding it out.

Cara touched it at another point and the same thing happened. She glided her hand along the material, turning it to stone as she did so and as she moved on, the stone walls transformed back into canvas behind her. Cara felt mesmerised. She walked round the room, slowly, touching, watching and feeling. She forgot about the dense air and her difficulty to breathe for a while.

After a while the presence she had felt around her of other beings came back to her awareness and with that returned also her awareness of her compressed chest and once more she felt difficulty breathing.

She tried to see the other beings, or at least to feel them more clearly. They took on no shape or visibility, but she could feel their anger and beyond that anger lay intense fear. She could sense panic around her. Like the light in the room, the beings were neither light, nor dark, neither living nor dead. They were foggy, misty, unclear. A thought came to her mind, striking her heart with its cold touch. The thought petrified her. She wondered if the beings she sensed were the spirits of those who, like her, had followed the rider into this container and had been trapped there forever, eventually suffocating to their death. Or maybe they had died of fear and panic. Or maybe the rage of those stuck there killed those who entered. And they in turn became spirits of rage, waiting to inflict pain, fear and eventually death on any new arrivals.

The white rider had vanished and Cara felt she would not return. She had possibly not even set foot in this room, disappearing from Cara's sight at the entrance, giving her the mistaken image of an entry. Perhaps she had never existed. In this room Cara's thoughts and memories had become unclear and muddled too. She was no longer sure of herself or anything that came to her mind. Everything was vague and uncertain.

Cara forced her breath to slow down, forcing herself to return to a state of relative calm. She remembered Rinchen's wisdom for every unknown, every new experience or sight, "patience". "Wait and feel" she told herself."Don't let fear rise in your soul. Fear blinds the eyes and clouds the mind. Just be calm. What will be will be". She sat down in the centre of the room, closed her eyes, remaining alert and aware of her surroundings and started to wait.

She watched as fear started to rise from her stomach into her chest. She realised the fear would take over her whole body if she didn't keep it under control somehow. She slowed her breath down further, watching its slow movement in and out of her body, relaxing into its natural rhythm, letting go of all other thoughts.

The minutes went by, Cara watching her breath, gradually feeling calm and strength return back to her. As she sat there, it suddenly dawned on her that the answer was clear. The spirits had not died of suffocation, they had died of panic. Their fear of death had led them to their death. It was the fear of suffocation that had killed them, not the lack of oxygen.

She told herself "be calm. If you stay calm and keep breathing, the air will last and you will survive. If you panic, you'll die". She went back to watching her breath, feeling a little reassured and forcing the tiny bits of confidence she had had a glimpse of to stay and grow. She held the signs of confidence in her heart, speaking to it and herself, repeating whatever came to her mind that might help over and over. "You will survive, be calm", "you are meant to be here", "watch your breath, it is settled, it is deep enough" "you're alive". Over and over she repeated sentences that helped. With each repetition they grew stronger, transforming from passing glimmers of hope, to established thoughts, to strong beliefs.

Suddenly something grabbed her from the back of her neck. She could feel fingers digging into her flesh. The grip hurt. She tried to move away, to shake it off, to turn, but she found she was frozen in her place. She could not move at all. Her whole body felt like heavy lead, immobile, rigid. She felt pain and fear. She tried to cry out, but no sound came out of her open mouth. She thought "you're hurting me, you're hurting me, you're hurting me". She kept repeating "you're hurting me" in her mind, unable to think of anything else. Gradually the words started to release out of her mouth in a hushed, strained whisper. She continued repeating them, finding her voice a little more with each repetition, until at last she was shouting it out loud to the walls "you're hurting me".

The sound of her voice, the depth of her breath, the vigour and truth of her words filled her with strength. Her fear turned into anger, which in turn turned into some kind of beyond human strength. She grabbed the hand on her neck and removed its grasp with force, throwing it away from herself. She stood up turning to face her aggressor ready to fight. But there was nothing there. She was looking at empty space. The aggressor had left. She realised she had found her strength and courage in the face of danger and pain. She had found her own voice and spoken out her own truth. Her truth had given her strength.

She turned towards the walls around her and shouted at them with conviction "you don't scare me, let me through" and slowly, in a smooth flowing motion the canvas lifted, vanishing gradually into thin air. Cara was free to go.

Cara found herself in clear, light surroundings. There was still a vagueness about the place. She felt as if she was floating in mid air, in the middle of a cloud. She wasn't sure which way to turn, all directions looked the same. She decided to simply move forwards in the direction she was facing for the time being. The fog might lift, her surroundings might change. And anyway, what else was she supposed to do.

She went on for a while, she had no idea for how long, she could not even guess. It could have been a few minutes, or a few hours. Time had a vague, foggy quality here too. There was no clarity in anything at all. Her surroundings, the time, even her own thoughts and feelings had become vague. Somehow she was glad though. She felt as though she had taken part in a long run, one that had passed through varied terrain. She felt tired. She could feel the weariness in her bones and muscles. Her skin felt stretched tight. Her mind was weary too, thinking would have been an effort, she was glad for the blank emptiness housed in her head. And especially the break from feeling was most welcome, the numb, empty calmness that had spread over her heart, blanketing all turmoil, numbing emotions, covering up memories. She realised how much she had been taxing every aspect of her whole being. She recognised her need for a break and the vague fog was providing her with what she needed. She felt no need to grasp anything solid. She did not wish for a clear thought or emotion. Fog felt good.

She moved on, slowly, not feeling any urge to rush. Not needing to think or feel, to plan or even look around. Just moving forwards, one step at a time. There was nothing for her in any given moment except for the step she was taking at that instant. A monotonous, slow process. One that she welcomed and was comfortable with.

She noticed a slight shift in the colour of the air in the distance, as if stray drops of purple had mixed into the fog at random points. She could see the centre of each droplet, dark purple, from which its essence spread outwards. The purple reminded her of some deadly poison Tenzin had warned her against.

She moved on, not changing her direction, feeling a slight spike of curiosity rise within her. As she drew closer, she noticed the droplets increasing in number and density. Not far off she could see so many of them that the blank fog had turned into a purple dense cloud. Where they were overlapping, the purple colour was so dark, it was nearly black.

She could taste the droplets now. They had a strangely bitter taste. She felt the need to throw up. Her nose and eyes were burning. "It is poison", she thought. She looked back, wanting to return to where the fog was unencumbered by these drops of poison, but they had taken over the space behind her too. They spread out in all directions, as if they had descended from the sky down to cover the whole world.

She covered her mouth and nose with bits of clothing and strained her eyes as she moved on. She felt her mother's presence everywhere. She could hear her mother move, breathe, talk, she felt her mother's spirit touch her skin. It was as if her mother had condensed into these tiny droplets of purple poison and travelled across the distances just to be able to suffocate Cara. A feeling of desperation took over Cara's heart, a feeling that there was no escape and that she could not get away, no matter how far she travelled. Her mother would always suffocate her, burn her, poison her. She remembered how months ago she had realised that to grow and become whole she would need to understand her mother, to get to know her. That time had come. The poison had a message and she needed to hear it.

She focused her eyes on the nearest cluster of droplets. They were moving and spreading. Their density and darkness increasing fast. In parts the purple had turned into black.

Darkness was gradually taking over the whole area. Soon it would be pitch black. There would no longer remain any light anywhere.

"Light", that was it. As soon as she thought of the elimination of light, she also realised what the answer was. She needed to bring light into the darkness and illuminate the shadow. Light would help clear the air, counteract the poison, lighten the droplets. "That brings me back to the beginning" Cara thought. Light would shine through with her understanding of the poison. But what was she to understand?

She settled to watching the droplets as she walked, moving very slowly forwards so as not to miss any detail. She watched the way they moved and interacted with each other, moving together, coalescing, then separating once more, in an unending dance of death. Big droplets gobbling up the smaller ones and then spitting them back out. Forms growing larger, then smaller. But throughout it all one movement prevailed. The purple clouds were growing in density and darkness overall. They were becoming larger and fuller.

The air became increasingly harsh. It was more burning, more stingy. Her nose, throat and chest burned. She was struggling to breathe, each breath hard to catch, and yet when caught, the breath itself was burning her. Her heart was aching with the effort. Her limbs felt heavy, dense and stagnant. Her whole body and soul wanted to lie down and give up, to find peace and rest in unconsciousness. But she dragged herself on, forcing one step after the other. She started to choke.

Just a little further she noticed a movement on the ground, or what she imagined was the ground, nothing but dark purple fog was visible to her in all directions and the ground had vanished beneath the fog. She could feel it under her feet, but she could not see it.

She recognised the movement. It was the slow, smooth, gliding motions of a snake. Just as she was reaching it, she noticed more snakes around her. She was surrounded by them. They broke the monotony of the dark purple fog. The fog stood stagnant and still compared to their slimy, oscillating movements. The fog was quiet in the background with the snakes hissing to cover up the deadly still silence that swallowed all other sound into its blanket stillness. Only the snakes were audible.

She tried to remember what she had been taught about snakes and what they meant. Snakes were ancient symbols of life, death, regeneration and deep wisdom. New life could come only through the death of the old. And snakes renewed themselves every year, shedding their old, worn skin, and bringing to the surface shiny, new, fresh skin.

What did snakes mean to her personally? Why had so many of them suddenly appeared before her? Why were there so many of them in her mother's presence? She hadn't really ever thought about them, except that one time when she had watched a snake shed its skin. But that had been different, that was a specific action, carrying its personal message, which had fitted in with her life and the point she had reached during her journey at the time. Now the scene she saw was different. Some of the snakes were hissing, moving around, curling up, lashing their tongues, some lay curled up sleeping, some raising their heads in a threatening manner, some moving to their own rhythm oblivious to their surroundings, some spread out, some in close contact with others. None of them were especially big, or looked especially dangerous, but together, so many of them did create a sense of menace. There were enough of them to build a whole army. Together they could have overwhelmed even the strongest, largest animal.

Their movements were so smooth and strong, it would take only an instant for one of them to strangle her. Even a hard tap with one of their tails would knock the life out of her. She could not understand their dance and stood in their midst, bewildered and confused.

Cara was shaken out of her reverie with a sudden, sharp stab in her ankle. She looked down, jerking her foot up at the same time. She saw a snake glide away with ease. Her ankle was bleeding. It had bitten her. Her ankle was stinging and blood was gushing out of the wound. She pinched around the bite to help push the blood out just in case it had been poisonous. She noticed the blood she forced out contained small purple clots, similar to the droplets all around her, but denser, more jelly like. She gathered some blood on her fingers and palm to look at it more closely.

The purple clot was moving autonomously, pulsating seperatly from her blood cells, but mingled together with the droplets in her blood stream. It was contracting and expanding, contracting and expanding, like a single cell animal, like the droplets in the air. Its movements were slow, but rhythmic and it moved in its place, without moving forward in any one direction. Cara wondered whether her whole body had been infused with these things. Had they entered her from the air she was breathing? Through her nose, mouth and skin? Or had they moved into her blood from the snake bite. Had the snake transferred poison into her body in the form of purple droplets? Did the snakes perhaps have the poison in them? Were they the creators, or the carriers, or just messengers, moving the droplets from one being to another? Would she, if she lingered here for long, turn into a purple animal, purple poison circulating through her body? Or would she die before it got to that?

She looked around her and saw that the air was already much darker. Breathing had become much harder and the pain in her ankle was increasing. She had a feeling her time was running out. Her instincts called out "hurry, hurry, HURRY!" And yet she could only wonder, "Fine, but hurry where, how, doing what?"

Cara needed to find out more about the snakes. She felt she'd find some kind of understanding, an insight into this mess through them. She needed to understand to survive. She strained her eyes, trying to take in the sights around her. The snakes all looked the same. She wanted to find the same snake that had bitten her, but she could not tell them apart. She wondered if it mattered which one she learned from, they were all aspects of the same being, they carried the same message, they were different elements of the same symbol.

She chose a sleeping snake, only because it was going to be much easier to capture. She held the snake close to its head and very tight. The snake woke up by her grip. It started to wriggle and hiss furiously, but it could not get away. Its tongue was lashing at her hand, not quite able to strike it.

Staring at it Cara wondered what she had been thinking when she decided to pick the snake up? What was she going to do with it now? She would not kill it, dissect it, or harm it in any way. What was there to see on its skin, in the movements of its thrusting head, furious, ready to bite, ready to strike her down? She could not analyse its insides without killing it and she would never do that. She had created fury in an angry, defensive, venomous snake, its anger turned towards her, the perpetrator. Too afraid to let go of it, too confused to know what to do with it, she stood still, watching, barely breathing.

As she stood there, her mind wondered, her focus lost intensity and her grip loosened for a moment. Taking advantage of an absent minded moment of hers the snake bit her hand. The surprise and sudden pain she received jerked Cara out of her reverie, her hand releasing the snake instantly. The snake wormed away with surprising speed and dexterity. Cara watched after it, making no attempt to recapture it. It was moving too fast for her to follow.

She looked down at her hand. She would need to learn all there was to learn from the new bite she had received. She pinched around the bite as she had done before and saw the blood oozing out, red at first. But then as it continued to flow out, a few purple droplets started to appear, then more, until gradually they were spread all around her blood.

She stretched her skin in various parts of her body trying to see if there were any signs of purple underneath. She saw none. The snakes did not look purple either. They did not seem at all burdened by the poisonous air surrounding them.

"My blood is not contaminated" she thought, "the contamination is around me. I let the poison in by inflicting harm on myself and then seeing the wound and the contamination, I am tricked into thinking that the whole of me is poisoned" She thought of her life and realised the significance of this realisation. All her life she had looked at her immediate surroundings and judged herself by the people around her, their opinions of her and their responses towards her. She had always judged herself harshly, guided by their unforgiving, limited judgements. Any negative situation in her environment and she would take the blame upon herself or contemplate her role in the incident. The world being imperfect as it was, she had always been able to find plenty of negative to take on. And she had dismissed the truth that people are not perfect either, none of them are and the more imperfections a person carries, the more they judge and label others, in the hope that their faults will go unnoticed in the commotion.

A person who cannot accept his weaknesses, his faults, his complexes, will place these on others. He cannot own, so he forces his baggage on to someone else so that they carry what he will not. And for long, Cara had been the unconscious carrier of all that her mother and those close to her did not want, could not own. She had been led to believe that all they gave her to carry was hers from the start. She had tried to change herself from within, but they could not be satisfied. They had not changed, their problems were still alive, so they continued to place them on Cara. And Cara took their poison on.

She not only took the negative on, she let these negative attitudes spread throughout her being, owning them completely, thinking they said all there was to know about her, mirroring one bad comment and spreading the image to encompass the whole of her. She judged and criticised herself unforgivingly. Any criticism of herself coming from the outside, she took on willingly, making it a part of her, even when it was wrong or unjust. Any mishap and she decided she was to blame, she searched for her role in the incident, owned the blame, felt the guilt and extrapolated that she was a terrible person, in need of punishment, unworthy of forgiveness.

She forgave others easily, but never herself. She demanded perfection from herself, even though she knew no such thing existed.

She saw now that the poison was in the purple droplets, linked in with her mother and the poisonous environment her mother had brought her up in. Any wound Cara inflicted on herself or allowed another to inflict on her, would be contaminated by this poison, which would then increase the size of the wound and the damage caused by it. But, Cara thought "it is not me that is poisonous, the purple is not in my veins, it comes to me from the outside, it is not mine and I will own it no longer"

Cara felt the need to name the poison, to help separate it from herself and give it an individual identity. She felt her mother's presence in it, so she named it "devouring mother". It had after all been created by her mother and her mother's bitterness, unhappiness and resentment. The harmful, deadly spite her mother exhaled. The devouring mother received strength from society and its labels and judgements of people. The devouring mother fed on the good and pure, on the strength of others, reached through a blind spot, a point of weakness.

The poison existed everywhere, whether covered over in a small community, whether in the burning of her chest when walking alone or as laws and morals in larger groups. As soon as people got into groups, they needed to assert opinions, make themselves part of something and make themselves look better than others, which usually meant finding a way of making another worse than themselves. People intuitively know they are not perfect, so if they cannot face, see and own their imperfections, they will hide or crush them. But knowing somewhere in their beings that the shadow is there, they won't feel comfortable in their own skins. To ease their discomfort and avoid facing their own imperfections, they label others as bad, finding in others' mistakes or downfalls an excuse to lift themselves higher, feeding their corrupted, misguided egos and making themselves feel better at another's expense. They search for an apple to punch, so that they can watch it bruise and rot and then they can stand beside that apple, in comparison looking ripe and healthy.

And her mother, the archetype, the impressive mountain of an example, the one in action, placing her poison full of resentment and evil on those around her. Her mother was not capable of seeing herself. She had no awareness of her actions or the way she led her life. She had no experience of what genuine truth was, the type of truth that reached out from the heart, that was pure and laced each word and action with honesty. She had to ignore the shadow, disown it, push it away. She had to place the shadow on others and Cara had been nearest, most available, easily within her reach. That way her mother could hold on to her idea of light and push the shadow into someone else, thinking that left her clean and unburdened.

But the shadow is there and cannot be denied. Hiding it, squashing it, ignoring it, refusing it does not destroy it, it only becomes stronger, more dangerous, growing off of denial daily in the dark recesses of the person's soul. Until one day it erupts.

Cara felt hatred towards her mother. She wanted to fight the feeling. It felt wrong to hate her own mother. She had been taught any negative feelings or actions towards one's mother were wrong, sinful, evil. But she could not deny what she felt. The hatred was there.

Cara hesitated, then succumbed. "It is my truth and I will embrace it" she thought. "I hate you" she whispered, "I hate you. How dare you try to kill me? How dare you take my life away from me? How dare you steal my ability to feel joy?"

Cara felt these truths and felt also how she had been short changing herself. She had been so unfair on herself, so harsh and demanding. Asking the impossible, then punishing herself for not achieving it. She had been under the influence of the devouring mother and had contributed to her mother's theft of her soul and life.

She started to cry. Hot tears rolling down her cheeks fast, like a river that had burst its banks after a long period of forced containment. The pent up pressure exploding, its strength impossible to stop. She cried till there was no liquid left in her. She cried till the burning in her mouth and throat had gone, her nose was soothed. She cried till her chest opened, so that she found her breath flowing freely once again. Her heart was beating savagely and life had entered her body once more.

She bent her head over her hand and sucked into her mouth as much of the purple, contaminated blood as she could. Then she spat it out. "You're not mine" she shouted out to her surroundings, "you are not mine. I will not house you".

She felt the pain in her ankle and hand easing, as if the blood was lightening, the poison withdrawing, the wound healing. Looking down she saw the skin closing up around the bite wounds. The snakes were moving away from her, slithering into the distance. She noticed a ray of light ahead, descending through the purple clouds, splitting the fog, with a spark of freshness and clarity.

She noticed a smile spread from her heart to her lips, eyes and face.

Cara walked towards the light, feeling lighter inside, but not yet entirely settled. The clouds around her were less dense and there was more light and movement in the air, but the fog hadn't blown away completely and still the stingy smell of poison lingered on in the air. She had brought enough consciousness to the droplets to allow some light to break through, but her work here was not yet done.

She reached up to a purple droplet and to her surprise she captured it easily in her hand. For some reason she had imagined they would be evasive. The droplet felt heavy in her hand. As she held it, she felt her arm start to feel heavy. Gradually her vision darkened. It felt like her whole chest had filled with some kind of heavy, dense liquid, like the one she was holding in her hand perhaps.

She felt a growing desire to give up on life, a feeling that her whole journey was futile, her effort pointless. She felt a yearning for death rise up within herself. She wanted to give up, lie down and never wake up. She wished she could die easily, without experiencing pain. Her arm felt like lead. She could not move it. She wondered whether she was breathing at all. If she was, it was shallow and slow.

Cara felt a sense of panic rise in her. She was suddenly afraid of the droplet. It was too heavy for her, too powerful. She wanted to let go of it. It was too dark and weighed too much for her to carry. She marvelled at its effect. That small droplet had taken over her so completely and so quickly, how could she have thought she might be able to deal with a sky full of them. She needed to get rid of it, but she found she had lost the ability to will her fingers open. She had no strength, she could not be bothered and once again she found herself thinking "what's the point anyway".

She collapsed to the ground, the droplet still in her palm, her fingers frozen, clenched around it, grasping it, not able to let go.

"I give up" she cried, "I can't go on. I give up. Let me go, let me die"

Cara watched her arm. She could feel the droplet suck all life out of her, and with her life, any ability to feel joy, any energy to move or live, all will to survive, any strength to even try. With these, all understanding of beauty was being drained out of her being. As it sucked further, so it gained strength and was able to take more. As the droplet grew in strength, Cara weakened. Her entire life and soul being sapped out of her by this poisonous little death cell.

A part of her mind was telling Cara to let go of the droplet, to shake it away and get up and move on. But Cara felt it was too late. "It has taken everything away from me, everything, there's nothing good or worthy left to go on with and no will or hope left in me to move"

Cara felt her chest contract into itself. She was losing the ability to breathe. She gasped for air. As she gasped, there was a sudden jerk through her body and her hand stretched open, releasing the poisonous dark purple droplet. Cara felt as if her chest had been torn out. She was gasping for breath, each effort painful, hurting her chest. Her chest started letting in air once more in spite of the pain. The droplet rolled away and she was breathing.

Cara lay where she was. She had no strength, but worse than that, she had no desire to move. She felt no hope. She felt low in spirit, a cloud of purple black depression had descended upon her and her body was saturated with it. "I have lost" she muttered, not aiming her voice at anything. "I'm alone and defeated. There's no reason to go on"

Cara lay there, wondering why she was alive, what the point of her ridiculous life was. She felt dark through her whole body and soul and she saw only darkness around her. All life had left her. She wondered if the potential for life had left her too.

At one time, not so long ago, yet it felt like an eternity away, she had been sure the potential for joy had left her, but she had had glimpses of it since. Would this shift too? Was it terminal or temporary?

Even her mind struggled. Thinking was too much. She gave up on following thoughts through and let her mind go blank.

The darkness she felt inside herself was intense. Her eyes closed, the world around her became dark. Nothing she would do would succeed, nothing would ever be good enough. She was not strong enough, her spirit did not hold enough light. She herself was darkness. She felt doomed to fail. The weight of darkness crushed down on her.

Just as she was passing out she felt somewhere deep within her a sense, a knowledge, a certainty, that this too would be pass. Like a whisper from God, a whisper that travelled from the depths of her heart outwards, she knew these clouds would leave her and light would return eventually. She still could not move, but she didn't feel the need to. All she needed to do was wait it out, like waiting for bad weather to pass. She willed some element of calm into her heart. She held on to the thought, the hope that the purple black cloud would leave her. With this thought lingering in her mind, she lost consciousness.

She saw white clouds in her dream, uncontaminated by any poison, floating with ease, basking in and reflecting out glorious sunlight. They were speaking to her in gentle, harmonious notes.

"You faced the Death Mother, Cara, and you have survived. Part of that confrontation though is what you feel now. The Death Mother sucks all life out of its victims. She is destructive and all-consuming. She is a strong force, grabbing all in her reach and sucking them into her dark vortex. She is death, although she lives on life. She is a dark, depressing, black hole, most do not dare face her, they seek to avoid her. They deny her existence and change direction when their time of confrontation is near. But your path lies through her. You need to see her, experience her, know her, recognise her and feel her before you can fully own all that you are and be who you are to be"

Cara dreamt of water, things flowing naturally with ease. The image provided such a contrast to the stagnation of the dense clouds. Water brought life and it contradicted the feeling of death she had been feeling, within and all around her. Water flowed, flushing out stagnation and deadly stillness. The image lightened her sleep. Water, flowing freely, bringing life back into stagnation, flushing away blockages. She allowed her mind to flow with the water, letting it cleanse her, washing away the poison.

Cara remembered the guidance she had received, again and again, "Accept, don't fight or struggle. Accept, feel and be. Even if it is death and heaviness you feel. Feel it fully. Don't be afraid, don't turn away from it. It is as much a part of life and truth as light is. You need to accept them both to be whole."

She reassured herself, "I have survived so far, the poison will flow off me with time. It is not mine to carry. It is there only for me to see and taste, so that I may understand. It is my path and I am supported in my journey. It cannot harm me if I let it pass over, rather than holding on to it and clutching it to make it mine"

She dreamt of evil spirits, trying to harm her as she lay unconscious and immobile. And every time they got close to harming her, some stronger, pure spirit rose from within her. She prayed to the spirit and to God and each time her prayers flushed the evil spirits back. They did not vanish, they held back, regrouped and returned. But each time Cara found it easier to send the evil spirits away. Her prayers came more easily, her heart grew livelier and each time, her prayers became fuller, more real, more heartfelt. The spirits grew weaker as Cara's heart strengthened and eventually they were defeated. They vaporised into thin air. Cara felt a deep sigh rise from within her body and she fell into a deep, peaceful sleep, her brow smoothed, her lips softened by a barely perceptable smile.

Spider webs in caves

The Caves

I stand alone in dark caves,
I think I do, but my body remains behind
My body lies still, rigid on the ground
I am disconnected from my body,
Separated, we are no longer one,
We are not linked in any way.

The caves are dark, so dark,
A chill, cold air blowing through them,
Who knows from where,
There are no openings, no cracks
Nothing air can breathe through
It blows and chills to the bone nonetheless
It is the breath of death,
Cold, powerful, indestructible

Death and decay everywhere,
No light or warmth,
No sign of life,
Only death

Cobwebs dangling loose from the ceiling,
Their spiders long gone,
Turned to dust and dirt
The smell of rot, of mould
And of cold, damp air

Shadows appear, all encompassing,
Dark, long shadows,

Full of secrets, full of the unknown
The shadows are more real than the walls,
More than the cobwebs, deserted by life
The shadows are more real than my own body
I can feel the touch of the shadows
On my being, caressing me
I could swear they were material
Of this world
I know they are not
Neither am I
I'm connected to the black shadows
Not to any living cell,
Not to flowing blood

I feel no fear, death is real
Death is fine
I don't welcome it, or shy from it
It just is

A thought comes to me,
Maybe after this there will be life,
rebirth, blossom, growth, green
Maybe in a moment I will see it, feel it
Feel alive and blooming
I hope.
Does not death result in rebirth?
But neither death
Nor rebirth ever come
Only the shadows remain.

Cara found herself facing the entrance to a dark cave. She felt slightly timid, she did not like caves. But she was curious at the same time and she realised she wanted to enter the cave, she needed to look into its darkness. Slowly she approached the entrance. It was pitch black inside. She looked around her for some source of light. There were a few trees to its left. She searched for some bracken and a long branch on the ground to light a fire. Once she had enough fire going, she lit the end of the branch and holding it up in front of her as a torch, she entered the cave.

The cave was damp inside, with cold, stone walls, covered in dead moss. There was no sense of life in there. Just a mouldy, damp air, nothing but darkness, damp and decay. The cave itself smelt of death. Cara moved on, feeling the cave's dead, stagnant, mouldy air within her body.

She reached a wide, high opening in the cave. The walls here were smooth, as if strong water flow had eroded their sides and ceiling, polishing them into a smooth, shiny surface. It was a large opening, yet she felt claustrophobic standing in it. She felt the walls caving in on her. She steadied her breath to regain control over her nerves.

She saw spider webs dangling from the walls all around her. The webs had decayed, bits of them hanging off loosely. She inspected a few of them, but saw no signs of life. "Even spiders have not survived this place", she thought. She sensed that they, and any other creatures that might have inhabited this space, had died a long time ago. Fear started rising from her stomach, but she pushed it back down. "I'm meant to be in here" she told herself, wanting to trust her instincts and where they led her, trying to force down doubt through the will of her statement.

She felt death all around her, the ultimate yin. Spiders, archaic symbols of engrained morals, rights and wrongs, surviving through generations, rigid and unquestioning. Morals created and accepted by all gatherings and societies, forced on individuals, allowing no space for autonomous thought and feeling led being. Squashing the individual, its personality, creativity, uniqueness. Taboos forcing engrained ways of living on all without any understanding of each individual's differentness. Strict, limited values, stagnant, without genuinity or true honesty. Impressions and dogmas of hopes and dreams, of what life should be, placed on individuals by others, who do not understand their nature, who live by written rules rather than by ways true to themselves and felt from the heart. Definitions for all aspects of life, love and happiness. These forced ways defining their lives for people that are so far from ways that could truly bring peace, love and joy. Cara thought about how these archaic rules related to her own life and how they governed her choices. In what ways had she forced them on herself without even realising it?

Cara's fear was gaining the upper hand. She could feel it rising in her towards panic. "Faith, have faith" she thought. She started to pray, in a whisper at first, then louder and louder. Praying to God for renewed faith, for courage. She tried to feel her heart, directing her prayers to her heart and trying to pray from her heart.

At first she could not feel her heart, she needed to imagine it. She focused on an image of her heart created as a focal point in her chest. It felt empty and dead, but she guided prayers, light and love towards that point. She forced her attention to where her heart was housed. After continuing to pray for a while, she felt stirrings in her heart. Her heart started to gradually thaw and come alive. As her heart woke up, the panic she had felt started to recede.

She felt the power of death lessen. She imagined those archaic, fundamental rules falling away from her being, like a garment no longer wanted, a robe no longer needed. Her heart felt lighter and stronger. "My true nature lies in my heart" she thought, "not in the garments placed on me by society. All that is not me, not my true nature is falling away like old, outdated garments". She imagined a vibrant flower covered with tattered pieces of old cloth. The flower started to come alive and the old garments fell away from it one by one, crumpling on the ground and disintegrating as they lay there. When the last piece of cloth fell away from the flower, it burst forth, a vibrant cacophony of colour and life. "Like that flower, my true nature is vibrant, full of colour and life. All I need to do to bring it out so that it can live and thrive is to release these old garments off of me". She felt a glowing light in her heart awaken. She felt the presence of God in her own heart, filling her heart, her body and spreading out from her being in to the universe.

She felt God speak to her, "I am". She was struck by the simplicity of the statement. God did not say I am this or that, I will do this or that, or even you do this or that. God spoke to her from within and without and simply stated the one universal truth "I am" Just that, just that God is. Not God is good or light, or any other descriptive word. God is. That was it. A simple, basic sentence containing the whole universe within it. She knew God was within her, as part of her, and more than all the parts of her put together. God was around her, pervading the whole of the universe and beyond.

Her heart felt pure and clean with the sense of connection. The glow of God's light started to spread up through her and outwards. Her whole body felt alive. She could feel every single cell in her body vibrate, tingle move. Every cell within her was coming alive.

The light brought joy and this joy filled her whole being. Gratitude, like warm larva started to spill out of her heart. Cara felt grateful to be alive. She prayed her heartfelt thanks, brimming to the top with new found energy and a desire to move on, to experience more and feel fully.

"This is who I truly am" she thought, "not the poison, not the darkness, not the depression, not my mother. I am this pure, glowing, vibrant light, with my heart as my centre. My heart is the centre of my being and my connection to God, the universal God that is all beings, living and dead, and God as my essence"

She remembered an old tale that Tenzin had told her. At the end of the tale, after much travelling, hardship and suffering the heroine had reached dark caves hidden away from most. Too hard to get to and little known, so that few ever reached their entrance. There the heroine met a giant spider, an archaic, feminine symbol of death, of a creature that draws life out of those that are living, absorbing their life into itself until they are sucked dry and dead. The spider lived on the life essence of all those that entered her cave. She bit them unconscious and then ate her victims alive. She did not kill them before consuming them, she needed to have them alive. Like the Death Mother, the spider needed to feed on life, to take and destroy all life. Others' lives fed her own life.

The heroine of the story was nearly devoured by the spider, but she was in the end saved by her faith. She had had courage to face the spider and she needed faith to survive it. Unquestioning, undoubting belief and faith in her cause and a hope that can only rise out of such complete belief. Understanding fully the reasons and mechanics did not matter. The details, no matter how big, were irrelevant. She was not clouded by doubts or questions. She reached her goal through her courage and her faith in her path and the absolute reassurance of God's presence in herself and all around her.

Cara felt she had reached the same stage on her own journey. Her spider was dead though, the webs decaying. She had moved beyond the rules of the world, beyond society and its restraints. Cara felt that the rest of her journey was to be the last phase of it and that it would ultimately lead her to her goal. She felt that it could only be completed if she held on to her faith and prayed for courage, qualities that emanate from the heart, the very centre of her being that was so defended and protected, surrounded by steel and lead and guarded against everything, good or bad, at all costs. She needed to keep her connection with her heart alive, feeding it with prayer and gratitude. In turn it would give her courage and strength.

Cara walked slowly back out of the caves into the sunlight. She lay down on the ground, looking up towards the clear blue sky. She carried the sense of joy within her still. She felt serene, content with life, happy throughout her whole body. She felt a sense of completion and achievement.

The baby

Cara moved on slowly, not taking in much of her surroundings. The energy to face new adventures had left her. She had a strong desire to lie down and go to sleep for as long as possible, but she knew she had to go on. Some unknown force within her kept her going, moving her legs for her.

One night, when she was feeling especially restless and disturbed, Cara had another dream. In her dream she was her father's child, but her mother's step child. Her parents had a son, a baby that belonged to them both. Her sister was her mother's, but not her father's. Cara watched her parents playing with her half brother. They showed him so much love. They played games with him, smiled at him, held him, were patient and caring with him and obviously enjoyed his presence. Cara thought "even my father never treated me with so much love".

In her dream Cara was told that her father could not have loved her, because her step-mother had been jealous of her and her father's love for her as a baby, so her step-mother had killed that love, destroying any threat the baby might hold for her husband's love towards herself. Her step-mother hated Cara.

But as Cara watched them play with the baby, the baby suddenly seized her father's neck and strangled him. Cara ran over to her father, finding him dead. She held her father in her arms crying and her father transformed into a little dead baby in her arms.

Cara was stricken by terror and dropped the baby to the ground. A scream rose up in her chest, but got stuck in her throat, she could not scream. She was overcome by grief and ran away from the scene.

Cara woke up with a jerk. She still felt the stuck scream in her throat. She felt grief and terror seize her chest. She got up quickly, needing to move, wanting to run away from the scene in her head. Her whole body was taken over by grief, terror and dread.

She spent the rest of the night sitting with her arms gathered around her knees, rocking forward and back gently, trying to soothe her spirit. It was striking that even though in her dream she was not her mother's blood daughter, the treatment of that mother, who hated her so openly and had no duty to love her or take care of her was the same as the treatment she had received from her own, real mother in real life. "Did she really hate me so much?" she wondered, and "why?"

In her dream her father was killed by the object of his love. Cara didn't understand what that might symbolise. Tenzin had told her once that all the characters in a dream are different aspects within the dreamer. But then what did the baby and her father in this dream symbolise within her? What part of her being was killing the object of its love?

How deep the pain lies
The wound that won't heal
It aches and screams
Deep below skin, invisible from outside

The mould eats away
Consuming cells, heart and lungs
It spreads in the night
Taking over the mind

In the morning it retreats sometimes
A fake dawn, a peace that is a lie
Some quiet, a serenity though
Is enough for the wound to be heard
Breaking the silence with its pain

Betrayed, abandoned, isolated
Standing alone, a forlorn figure
Watching the tide ebb away
Just as it is with life

Cara walked on as soon as there was enough light to see by. She could not bear to stay still any longer. She knew she needed to understand her dream, but she felt the answer could only come if she kept moving. If not an answer, at least a way of finding the answer would become obvious if she moved on. But if she stayed still and waited, inspiration would stagnate also.

Presently she came to a tiny hut, standing isolated in the middle of desolate, empty terrain. The hut was derelict, it looked abandoned. Cara knocked and waited. No sound reached her ears. She knocked again. She waited for a few minutes, then she pushed the door open. It was dark inside and airless. It had been shut up for a long time. There was an atmosphere of expectation in the room, as if it had been waiting. There was mould on the walls and the hut was showing signs of decay.

Suddenly the door slammed shut behind her. Full of fear Cara ran to the door, but it gave in easily to her push and opened, letting in the outside air and light. Cara looked outside, but there was no sign of anyone there. There was no sign of life in the hut either. "It must have been the wind" she thought, but the air was deadly still, not even a slight breeze moved the air. Perplexed she looked around again, but finding no solution, she gave a deep sigh and tried to push the fear, still lingering in her body, near the surface, close to panic, down. "It was nothing, just a sudden gust of air" she repeated to herself, not really believing it, but hoping the words would calm her taught spirit.

She looked around the room again. The room looked like it had been frozen in time. Cara felt a chill run through her body. "The warmth to defrost it will come from your heart" she thought and tried to feel her heart, but could not. She imagined hot lava flowing down a mountain, melting all in its path, melting frozen stars and frozen huts and frozen hearts. But as she imagined it, the lava froze mid stream, waves of lava frozen in space, still gold and red, but immobile, frozen into stillness.

Cara walked out of the hut, the sensations of cold and death within it were too overwhelming for her to stay with any longer. She needed the support of the sun. While she had lingered inside, the sky had clouded over and the sun was no longer visible. It was cold outside. Cara felt small, insignificant and afraid. She felt she had to move on.

She left the hut behind with a burdened heart. She had left without resolving whatever it had wanted to bring to her attention, but she didn't think she'd find a resolution if she stayed. She didn't have enough energy in her body to warm her limbs. Her blood was struggling to flow through her cold veins. She was afraid that if she stayed any longer, she would freeze in that place, or become one with the mouldy, decaying walls. She needed outside warmth and strength to thaw her body and help life energy flow through her freely.

She walked on for a while, feeling cold and distressed, her mind wandering randomly, not able to settle on any one thought or image, too dazed to focus or think.

She came across a woman, sitting comfortably on the ground, with a slight smile playing on her lips. Cara suddenly realised that she was hungry for human companionship. She didn't want to disturb the woman, so she sat down near her, but leaving enough space between them so as not to crowd her. She watched the woman for a while, but her mind was still skipping around without focus or understanding and soon she forgot about the woman, lost in her own reveries.

She was jolted back to her surroundings by a firm, but gentle touch on her shoulder. The woman had stood up and walked over without Cara noticing. She was standing next to Cara, smiling down at her with her hand on her shoulder. Cara returned her smile and scrambled up to her feet.

They started walking side by side, without the necessity of a single word being uttered between them. No communication was needed except for their initial smiles. That had been enough. They had both known in that moment that they were combining their two separate journeys into one. They would continue together.

The woman's touch had communicated the answer to Cara's unclear question. Her mind had been so scrambled, she hadn't even realised there was a question lingering within her until that moment, when both question and answer appeared simultaneously. The warm touch of another being, the acceptance of one by the other without question, the wordless understanding between them, these were the outside forces that would warm her body and defrost her parents' rejection of her. It was possible to see, feel and find love anywhere. It was everywhere, all around, for those who could sense it. All Cara needed to do was to let it in. The warmth of the woman's touch had spread throughout her body, re-igniting hope and energy within her.

Her father was just a child, a lost soul on earth, like any other. He had made mistakes, like others, and misplaced his trust and affections, like many others. A child needed unconditional acceptance, as it was, without any limitations or judgements placed on it. Cara felt love towards her father and a deep, heart felt acceptance of him, in spite of their past. She pitied him and her pity turned into compassion.

Her mother had not felt the need to bind Cara by conventional loyalties and duties. Her treatment of Cara had always been akin to that of an evil step-mother and Cara needed to accept her as such. If she could let go of the desire and expectation of motherly love or affection from her mother, she would then be able to let go of resentment and anger too. Cara understood that for her mother Cara was the enemy, and that was her mother's problem to resolve, not Cara's. She did not need to carry that burden for her mother any longer.

The dream had been an insight into her parents' treatment of her and their places in her world, exaggerated, but essentially real and true. Staying with them, where they stood, frozen and dead, would lead to mould, stagnation and ultimately death. Cara was ready to move on beside this warm spirit that had appeared to support her on her journey.

Cara's new companion was taller than her. She was ageless, holding both a wise and old aura about her, as well as being full of youth and vibrancy. She had wavy blonde hair and blue eyes. She had a calm nature and a smile that seemed set into her countenance from regular use. She seemed to belong to the earth. She came from it, was nourished by it, trusted in it and understood it. Cara felt at ease in her presence. She had a calming, soothing effect on Cara and a positive attitude towards everything that was contagious.

They didn't talk much, but they didn't really need to. Few things needed to be communicated through words. Mostly a look, a smile, a glance was enough. What they said mattered. They did not need to waste energy uttering needless words for the sake of it or to fill in gaps made loud by insecurity and lack of confidence. When in silence, there was a natural understanding that flowed between them, that rendered words superfluous. Cara could tell what her friend was thinking and feeling and she knew this was reciprocated.

Her name was Norbu, jewel, and she had travelled far from her village like Cara. Unlike Cara, where Norbu came from people were gay, friendly, supportive and generally happy. She had left because she wanted to see more of the world and learn more about herself. Their aims, the direction they were taking and what they were hoping to find were similar, but their starting points could not have been more different.

They came soon to the side of a small, gurgling stream and started following it in the direction it flowed. Cara welcomed the cheerful sound of the stream having spent so long in barren wilderness. It flowed playfully, making light of its journey, laughing out at the world, carefree. Cara wanted to be like the stream, light hearted and joyful, free of burden and weight.

Norbu read her thoughts. "We must first find Kali" she said. Cara felt a chill of fear go through her. She wanted to stay by the stream, in oblivion, unaware of the rest of the world, unaware even of herself. She wanted a break from struggles and effort. But she knew she must follow wherever their paths led them. There was a reason for every experience that she encountered. Each event and image propelled her further along her way, teaching and guiding her, filling her with understanding and knowledge, bringing her closer to her goal. She could not turn away from any possibility brought to her attention.

Eventually they came upon a derelict site. They were surrounded by broken down huts. In every direction there were signs of destroyed life scattered around them. There was blood on the ground and smeared across the stones. Overused daggers had been left lying about. Huts were burnt or hacked down. Cara could still smell the putrid essence of death in the air. She saw no bodies though, living or dead.

Norbu wandered without hesitation towards the centre of this broken down, destroyed place, once inhabited. Cara was amazed at Norbu's lack of fear. Her own feelings were very different. Her stomach churned, she thought she would throw up. Her nostrils were full of the putrid, dense air surrounding them.

Norbu walked straight into one of the huts with easy, determined steps. It was the largest hut around, although destruction had left it much humbled. Most of the roof had caved in. There were signs of an old burned out fire across its walls. It looked like it might crumble down altogether at any moment.

There had been some kind of war at this site. Had the fighters all killed each other? And if so, where were the bodies? They could not have already decayed into the earth, the smell of death was too fresh.

She touched the wall of the hut. It was dry and bits crumbled off under her fingers. The earth around it was damp and she could see blood marks splattered on the lower parts of the walls and the earth below. A dagger lay at her feet. She picked it up. It felt heavy in her hands, solid, comforting as a potential protector. She followed Norbu into the hut, clasping the dagger with both hands.

She could not see her friend anywhere within. She should have been able to. Although it was dark inside, there was enough light to see by. Marks of fire and blood were all around her, but no sign of her friend. She called out in a loud whisper, not daring to make much noise. She could not have said why she tried to be quiet. Was she afraid of rousing spirits resting in that place, waiting for unsuspecting visitors, to pounce on them when they entered? She felt ridiculous, but still, she continued quietly. She received no reply from Norbu. Not even a small sound to suggest she was anywhere in the hut.

Cara turned to walk back out, but she already felt, even before she turned and saw it, that her entrance had been barred.

The sight that awaited her was terrifying. A looming figure of power stood at the entrance, alert and ready to strike, a dagger in one hand, a snake in the other. She had long curly black hair held back with a string of thorns and dead, dry branches. As terrifying as the figure was, she was also awe inspiring. Cara trembled before her, but more than fear she felt respect. She knew she would do whatever this menacing, dark female figure bid her do, not to protect her life, but because the figure demanded obedience. She bowed in front of this incredible figure. The woman spoke in a hushed, subdued, deep low voice, "you have arrived at last"

She looked up and saw that the figure was not threatening in her stance any longer, just watchful, reading Cara's moves and expressions. She lifted her head to try to see into her dark face. She understood that instant that she had found Kali.

She went down on her knees, bowing her head before this amazing force, an apparition of strength and power. Beautiful in her ugliness. Dark and yet glowing and luminous.

Cara waited, not knowing whether she should be expecting a blow to her neck, or some transforming miracle. She knew if she died she would receive new life and to receive new life, she needed to die. The thought of death didn't trouble her. Her mind was ready, yet her hands were shaking, her breath shallow and short.

Cara felt Kali's presence directly in front of her, towering above her bowed head. She could feel cold chills running up and down her spine. She dared not look up. Then she felt a source of light, as if the sun was shining a ray of warmth and light directly into her heart. A glow of confidence spreading through her limbs, bringing with it a desire to live. She felt her body strengthen, a flow of energy strong enough to fulfil her any will. Her fingers tingled with strength and pulsating blood flow. She saw the image of a lion appear in her mind. A lion with golden mane, shining like the sun, a symbol of extraordinary strength and pure, primal, animal energy.

Cara looked up, but Kali had vanished. Instead, her friend Norbu was standing at the entrance, looking down at her, smiling. Cara looked around but saw no sign of Kali. "Where is she?" she asked, her eyes burning into Norbu's, as if she might force an answer out of her by boring into her mind with her intense gaze. She needed to know. She wanted Kali back. The strength emanating from Kali, the all powerful and empowering energy flowing out of her had been pulled back too fast. Cara needed more.

Norbu replied "Inside of you"

Cara looked down, realising the truth of the statement. She could feel her heart burning hot, glowing, its warmth spreading out into her body like lava out of a live volcano. Her heart was pumping out life energy. Her protected heart had at last broken out of its shell and she could feel its warmth spread into every single cell throughout her body.

She noticed the blood around her once again. There was so much blood, some of it not even dry yet and some of it dry

182

for a long time. She looked around, in her imagination the blood coming alive, starting to move, squirming with pain, death and suffering.

She looked back up at Norbu, who hadn't moved from her spot. She was still watching Cara with her gentle, soothing eyes.

"Did she do this?"

At first Norbu shrugged, as if it didn't matter, or she didn't care. Then very gently she said "No. They did it to themselves."

Cara looked around once more. How could they have? And why?

Then she thought of her own village and the riders she had so deeply felt she belonged amongst. The riders spent most of their lives riding from village to village, leaving suffering behind them wherever they went, bringing starvation, loss and pain to those whose paths they crossed. They shed blood too, lots of it. In fact inflicting pain, blood and suffering were a part of their way of life.

She had seen and met women from other villages, who were just as abused by their circumstances as she had been by hers. Yet some of these women carried peace and the potential for happiness within them. Their communities were supportive and accepting, not bitter, angry, cold, resentful and unhappy like the people in her village. Did they choose their unhappiness? Did they pluck it out from amongst all of the potentials floating in the air and make it their own, while they could have just as easily chosen peace and happiness?

Cara thought of animals, people, wars. Shedding blood, spreading pain, killing and dying were a part of this world. They were the very essence of life on this earth. Love turning to hatred, ownership to loss, want to theft, hurt, pride to death. Every born creature died and every new life ended. Each chapter had a conclusion, each search a finding and everything found started a new search. Questions invited answers, and answers further questions. Sunlight brought with it shadow.

Day was followed by night and night by day. Life needed the warmth of the sun, but without cool air, night or rain, sun scorched and dried, killing all that needed it to live.

Suddenly Cara's blood froze in her veins. She could feel no warmth or movement inside of her. She had lost the glowing energy that had been emanating from within her only minutes ago. Her thoughts felt dark. She felt only the shadow and not the light. They were both there, so why was it so much easier to feel the darkness and forget that darkness needed light and was born out of light? Why could she not hold the two together? Why was it always one or the other?

She looked at Norbu once more "Why do people kill?"

Norbu smiled. "Are death and life not opposite sides of the same coin? They kill to live. And some live to kill. Shed blood flows into the earth and becomes new life, new blood. People kill because they disinherit their own shadow, they try to keep the darkness inside of them down, invisible, they try to suffocate their anger. Anger buried in darkness and trampled on becomes rage and grows into a demon, with a life of its own, taking control of those that tried to exterminate its existence, that tried to deny its truth. And this demon is capable of any evil and strong enough to put into action the holders' worst fears."

"So what do we do?"

"Shine light on the shadow. See it, accept it. Know it is a part of you that should not, can not be shunned. Do not turn from it, or be afraid, or ashamed of it. It is part of your truth and part of the whole. And the whole, with all that it is, with its light and shadow both, is beauty and love"

"I don't understand" Cara said simply. She was aware that the will to live that had invaded her whole body only a short while ago had completely left her. The concepts being thrown at her loomed above her, too big for her to hold, too evasive for her to grasp. "Why did she let me live?"

"She does not force death or life on anyone. Each makes their own choice. She only grants them their wish. You did not wish death, although you thought you did. You wished for strength to live. You wanted faith. You asked for support and love. So that's what she gave you"

"I don't understand" Cara repeated, in a low, weak voice. Her words were barely perceptible. Then, not much above a silent whisper she added "Why me?"

Cara sat on the earth. She remained at the exact spot she had fallen to her knees to in front of Kali. Her eyes were open, but not able to see her surroundings. The only thing in her vision was shed blood. She saw blood around her and within her, blocking all other sight. She saw the blood of the dead. Blood, which was a giver of life, had at that moment become nothing but a symbol of death to her.

When she finally did manage to shake herself out of her stupor, she saw that Norbu was busy lighting a fire. She moved over towards her slowly "Do we have to stay in this place of death?"

"Why not? It's as safe as any other. And anyway, it's getting dark and we could do with the shelter"

Cara felt too weak to argue. She didn't want to sleep there. She was sure she was inhaling death, taking in its cold energy. She didn't like being surrounded by the marks of fire and by all that blood, shed by those who were no longer breathing. But she followed Norbu's moves and helped her with the fire. The warmth of the burning wood was welcoming. The mystical, playful dance of the flames eased her heart a little. Soon she had fallen into a dark, dreamless sleep.

Cara woke up with a start in the middle of the night. She had been bleeding. She could feel the sticky wet of blood on her skin. She was lying in a pool of it. She moved her hair away from her face with her hand and felt the sticky fluid on her face. Her bloody hair had stuck to her cheek. "I must have had blood on my hand" she thought. She felt disgusted by the idea of having blood on her face and all over her body. She felt her entire life energy, her life essence had poured out of her in the form of blood.

"So what have I done to myself then?" she wondered. If all the blood in the hut had been the doing of the people themselves, how was she shedding her own blood? In what way was she robbing herself of her own life essence? How was she wasting it? How was she turning the very essence of life into this useless, disgusting, sticky fluid?

She felt panic rising in her chest and looked around for Norbu, but Norbu was nowhere to be seen. She cried out to her, but heard no sound in return.

She started inspecting her own body, searching for the source of the blood flow, the wound, opening, whatever it might be. She found nothing amiss anywhere on her body, only that it was covered in blood. "Is it even my own?" she wondered. She felt no pain, just disgust.

She wondered if she should run away and leave this cursed dark place, but her body had tightened up during the night. It was tense with the fear of the previous day and from waiting still in the cold night. She could not move. She had to wait. She had no idea what all this meant and where this night would lead her, but she felt sure she had to wait. She had to hang in there, with no guessing of the future, no understanding of it, no hope, simply waiting in darkness, in the unknown. "So tell me Tenzin, how do I accept this suspense, this long, continuous waiting in the unknown, for the unknown, in pitch black and cold?"

She felt rage rise up within her. Rage towards the world. Rage towards Tenzin who had taught her so much, then let her go when there was still so much more to learn. The wise woman who had taken up a seat in her heart, then shattered that seat and her heart with one terminal blow. She felt rage towards her mother who had forsaken her own child, her responsibility, one that she had asked for and taken on consciously. Rage towards her one love who had betrayed her love and broken her heart. Rage towards God for bringing her to this earth for no seeming purpose except that she might suffer her painful fate. Rage, pure rage. Rage towards Norbu for vanishing when she needed her most. What did Norbu know anyway, who was she? Rage, red rage and pitch black darkness. A rage that she was terrified of. A rage that could kill, that could explode and destroy the whole world. Pure rage spanning the decades, her entire life, spanning the continents, spanning all of space and time, all encompassing, pure and universal.

She screamed into the dark night, a scream of warriors, ready to strike. And as soon as the scream had left her, her terror started to take over. Rage and terror fighting for control over her body until she could take it no longer.

She broke down into heart breaking, thundering, convulsive sobs. She was crying so hard and so fast, she could not breathe. She started to gasp for air, but her chest had collapsed. Another scream was present in her chest, but this one was stuck, suffocating her.

Then she heard a soft scrambling sound behind her and the next instant she felt warm, comforting arms around her back and shoulders. Norbu was holding her tightly, rocking her gently, soothing Cara's poor ravaged soul. Cara cried herself to sleep, too fatigued to try and understand or to move or speak.

Darkness all around
Bats flying blindly
You can hear their frantic wings
They have no direction
No purpose other than to survive
Fear everywhere
Blind, frantic will to survive
To stay alive, not to really live
But just not to die

She lifts the spear
Sharpened only yesterday
It will cut, shatter, but not kill

After all, no death is desired
Death means an end
An end to inflicting pain
An end to her suffering
The victim must hurt and bleed
But stay alive
So that she can break her heart
Again and again and again

She lifts the spear
Aiming for the centre of her daughter's heart
She never misses
But they both know
The time is near
When her heart will be out of reach
It's only a step away
But the daughter fears
Who is she without the pain
What is life without the suffering
The spear is at least a presence
Without it, she is alone

She's been told there's plenty light
Grass, meadows, trees and life
She has had glimpses of beauty
But she is afraid to step out.

The spear hurts too much though
She tries to protect her fragile heart
Encloses it in a steel cage
Hoping she'll be safe
Within reach of its sharp blade
But out of harm's way
It's a fallacy though
The spear always gets her
Her heart always breaks

Blood gushing out
Even the blood can't flow freely
It's stuck in a container
Purple, poisonous, like the mother
Like the mother's jealousy
Her savage wish to kill
To destroy life
And the potential for life

When apart from her mother
She turns upon herself
The spear and broken heart
Are all she knows
She is afraid of venturing out
Losing her 'self'
The one she knows
The misunderstood victim,
The hurting girl
The struggling martyr
To be selfish
To move on
To take flight
These potentials fill her with fear
So she digs her heels deep
Into the murky ground
Stuck in darkness with the spear
And the hand that knows only destruction
Repeat repeat forever
Tears that roll down her eyes
But cannot flow freely, cannot release
Even liquid gets stuck in darkness
In darkness nothing can see
Nothing gets felt
All is a lie

Dark dark, everywhere is dark

Bats blindly frantic
Trying to survive
Wishing to die
Dark, like their eyes
That cannot see
Dark like the hand that holds the spear
Dark like the life that could not give
Dark like the mother who could not love
Dark as her disgust
Her hatred for her own daughter
Bitterness turning to evil
Evil into murder
And yet the poor soul lives
She fights and screams
Her screams are heard
Hands held out to lift her up
But like a blind bat
She struggles and fails
She beats around too wildly
Too blindly to get out
God will heal though
God will touch her heart
Her heart will glow and shatter the cage
Her tears will flow freely and feed the soil
The tree of life will grow and bloom
Boats will take sail
Butterflies fly
And her heart will beat
A living organism
Red with vitality
Unhindered and free.

When she awoke, Cara was still in Norbu's arms, only Norbu had fallen asleep too. "She sleeps like a child" Cara thought, "so innocent and at peace, like an angel"

She moved away softly and lit the fire with remaining bits of wood.

She walked out of the hut. A cool fresh breeze greeted her. The sun was shining through intermittent clouds. A sense of life had come back to the area over night. She could hear birds in the distance and her surroundings did not seem as gloomy to her as they had the night before.

She walked off a short distance, looking around her. Nothing seemed to have changed in her surroundings as such, but somehow the area did not feel as dead, as destroyed, as beyond salvation as before. There had been a shift in energy, in the earth, the air and even in the destroyed huts. Life had transformed somehow, the energy had turned around. The earth around her was coming out of its deadly non-existence. The sense of numb waiting had left the place, instead it had been replaced by subtle, barely perceptible movement and change. Growth had started underground, there would be shoots of green coming out of the earth in the spring. The breeze was clearing the air, cleansing away the stagnation. The mouldy, bloodstained smell of death was getting swept away, leaving a fresher scent in its stead. Life was returning to the valley. Life always followed death, fresh, new life out of surroundings that before did not seem capable of holding and bringing forward any living thing ever again. An energy that lifted beings out of their slumber.

Cara returned to the hut, feeling refreshed. Hope was rising inside of her. She felt excited about what the day would bring and her mind was filling with expectation.

Norbu was up and had managed to find some water which

she was heating over the fire. Cara realised how hungry she was. She had forgotten all about hunger and food the day before, but now she felt her empty stomach clamouring loudly to be fed. There was nothing in the pot though, just water. And she knew there was nothing to cook outside either. Her spirit fell. She wondered how long they could go on without food.

"How quickly your mood changes" Norbu laughed. "Don't worry, we'll find something soon. But first some hot water to warm our insides"

Once they had had drunk from the pot, they set off again, walking in a direction that Cara thought was probably randomly chosen by Norbu. But she wasn't sure. Norbu seemed to have a deep store of knowledge and intuition that Cara could not as yet fully fathom.

"Will we see her again?" Cara asked, her mind having returned to the dark goddess.

"I don't know. If we need her, perhaps"

Cara wondered at how accepting Norbu was by nature. She was happy with whatever turn their journey took. She was able to make the most out of each and every circumstance, without being drawn down into darkness or despair, without even being clouded with doubt and insecurity. She was full of faith and confidence. A natural ease with the way of the world emanating from her at all times. Whomever she saw, she took in, whatever she saw she learned from, without shirking away, without pushing away, without trying to hold and keep. Cara wanted to be like her, but she was still drawn towards and away from things. She still liked and disliked. She still felt anger, shame, preference, happiness and depression. She was gradually learning to be more accepting though. The sight of last night would have been too much for her to bear even just a year ago, yet she had born it, questioned it, thought about it, felt it and therefore also learned from it. But what? What had she learned?

Their surroundings gradually started to change. They could see the odd tree and odd plant appear here and there. It was all still pretty barren, but gradually small signs of life were appearing around them.

The sun was still shining, although the previously intermittent clouds were getting darker and more dense. Cara felt her hunger and tiredness acutely. She was running out of energy and wondered how Norbu was managing.

"Can we not try to eat one of these plants? Surely there's something we can do with them?"

Norbu looked a little withdrawn as she shook her head "No, they will not do, they are hallucinogenic, we would lose ourselves here"

"But there's got to be something. I can't go on any further"

"Just a little more Cara. We are nearly there"

"Nearly where? How do you know? Where are you taking me?" Her hunger and fatigue made her temper short. Cara's wish to rest and eat turned into resentment and impatience with Norbu. If she didn't know, then they should stop. If she did know, then why the hell was she not telling her? Why had she brought her here? "Some information would be nice", Cara thought. If Norbu was trying to prove her strength and equanimity to Cara, she had communicated her message clearly and Cara was fed up. Cara hated her suddenly. Her frustration and anger turning to the one person near her.

"I'm not going on. Why should I listen to you anyway? What do you know? I've had enough. Always so quiet. If you know something, tell me. If not, do as you please, but I'm staying"

Norbu looked at her for a moment. Cara found her gaze uncomfortable and turned her back on her. She heard Norbu move on slowly. She had decided to leave. Panic gripped Cara's heart. She felt the full blow of sudden solitude hit her, the fear of loneliness in this barren, unwelcoming environment, alone with her hunger and defeated heart. Fear broke within her then, but her spirit had already been broken. She sat down and started to cry. She had asked Norbu to say something. Norbu had chosen not to. Cara's pride would not allow her to run after her. She cried for a long time, feeling all her old heart breaks surface, triggered and brought back to life by this recent blow. She was alone once again. Abandoned once more.

She slept in the open and her dreams were haunted by voices "They did it to themselves" "It was their own doing" "You shed your own blood" "You are your own wounder" "You are your killer" "You are your deserter" "You get what you ask for"

All the voices were clamouring together, pointing out her guilt. She had caused her own pain. She woke up crying once more. How could she cry so much. How could there possibly be enough water in her to shed so many tears.

Then she remembered Kali's life giving touch, the warm lava spreading out of her heart.

She got up to her feet, although it was still dark. "I will go on. I chose to live, not die. And I am strong enough to go on. She could have spoken, she chose not to, it is not my fault she left"

She felt strength return to her limbs. She looked up at the stars. It had been so long since she had last read them. She watched them for a while, praying to them for guidance. When she noticed that the sparkling blinking of one star was stronger than the others, she decided to follow its direction. It had twinkled at her and she would pay attention.

She started walking towards the star, feeling her limbs become warmer with movement and her heart strengthen as a result of having an aim, a will to move, to do something. She felt the strength of action grow in her once again. She felt the energy that forward movement gave not only to her limbs, but also to her tired heart.

Rats

As dawn was breaking she noticed a change in the air. The gentle breeze was carrying a fresh scent with it. She felt hopeful. The scent suggested water and food. And sure enough, another half hour of walking brought her to a gathering of trees, clustered around a small lake. She could even hear a bird or two. She hastened towards the lake. She was thirsty. She cupped some water and smelt it. Then, not really caring about risks any longer, she drank heartily from the lake and washed her face. It felt so pure and fresh, she wanted to immerse her whole body in it.

The trees held fruit and an easy climb brought her high enough in the branches to gather some. She ate, then drank some more. She removed her clothing and entered the cool, fresh, glistening, clear water. It was bliss. The cool touch of clean water on her skin, the welcoming depth as she sank gently into its arms. The soft earth under her feet.

She enjoyed the water and its produce for a long time, happy to stay in this place of beauty and natural riches, unwilling to leave. She felt revived, energy returning to her fatigued body. She let out a deep sigh of contentment. If only she could stay by this lake forever. It was a quiet spot that welcomed her, where she had found all she needed at that moment.

But eventually she started to grow restless. There was not much to do or see and once she had recovered her strength, her mind started working. She thought about what she was to do next and where she needed to go.

She decided to continue in the same direction she had been walking when she found this serene oasis. She headed off, carrying as much fruit and water with her as she could. It wasn't long before she came upon a single hut, standing out alone in the barren wilderness, isolated and proud.

As she drew closer she noticed that it looked tired and worn down. She could see no sign of life anywhere around and the door of the hut was unhinged, swinging gently in the breeze. She stopped and called out. Receiving no answer, she walked over to the hut and looked inside. It was completely empty except for the remnants of a fire in one corner, extinguished long ago. A few shelves adorned the walls, cracked or broken, hanging loosely off their hinges.

She welcomed the idea of a night's sleep in a sheltered spot, next to a warm fire, so she decided to stay the night. She gathered some wood and bracken from near the lake and returned to the hut to make herself comfortable. Soon she had a crackling fire going. A sound that eased her sense of loneliness. She had grown accustomed to Norbu's presence and the solitude she now found herself in was in stark contrast to the support and companionship she had received from Norbu.

The fire was beautiful nonetheless. The flames dancing, igniting in her imagination tales of pretty lands, where fairies danced and sang, where life was joyful, lively and warm. Worlds where no one was ever left alone, no one ever shunned or cast away. Where women lived with their children, without the fear of losing them. Where no one fought and everyone laughed.

She laughed at her silliness and fancies. As improbable as they were, they had lifted her spirit and she welcomed rest. She lay down and slept in peace, with an easy heart and calm mind.

The next morning she noticed, as soon as her eyes opened and was able to take in light, that she was not alone. A rat was sitting directly in front of her face, not more than two paces away studying her with understanding eyes.

The rat, seeing that she was watching it, moved away a little and started gnawing at a piece of wood lying on the ground. It held the wood between its two paws and got to work on it full of concentration. Cara saw an image of rats everywhere, in her hair, all over her body, gnawing, gnawing, gnawing away at her. "No" she shrieked, "there will be nothing left of me"

She rushed up and shook her clothes. There were no rats on her. In fact there were no rats anywhere around her except for the one gnawing away at the wood. The rat stopped its work, on alert after Cara's rushed, startled movements. "You're like my thoughts" Cara told it, "my destructive thoughts that gnaw at me, creating disease and pain, obsessive thought patterns, eating away at my flesh. I think I can't get away from them, that they are all over my body, in my hair, but in reality they stand a few paces away, watching me as I absorb them completely"

The rat turned back to its piece of wood and started gnawing at it again.

"Go away" Cara screamed, "leave me alone. Go away"

Cara started to cry. There was a sense of panic and fear within her. She was in turmoil. Her chest contracted, her mind raging without focus, without comprehension. "What's wrong with me? There's something so deeply wrong with me. What is it? Why am I this way"

The raging turmoil continued. She could see the rat, but she was not able to focus on it. She wanted to scream, but there was no point. The rat ignored her, happy in its own little world. "Leave me alone" Cara sobbed. Tears had taken over her so fully, she could no longer see. She sobbed, covering her face. There could be no peace with such destruction raging in her.

Then she remembered the one word she needed to embrace most "accept". "Accept what?" she wondered. "Accept those thoughts are within you. Look at them. See that they are not the truth, so that you can knowingly let them go. See them as they are, separate entities, gnawing away apart from you"

"I want to be at peace" Cara thought, "I don't want any rats within me". But she also knew that wanting to get rid of the rats was the opposite of accepting them. She had to come to terms with the rats in her mind, accept their power, see their nature, accept that she must move forward with them, not by kicking them away, but by understanding them.

"What are rats good at?" She was fumbling in her mind, trying to find a way in, trying to find an avenue through which they would be other than gnawing destructive elements. She was searching for some positive way of viewing them.

"They're resourceful" she thought, as she noticed the rat find some soft flesh within the wood that it was chewing. It swallowed what it had found, evidently pleased with itself and content with its food. It had managed to find nourishment in this barren, forsaken land.

"They're finders. They can survive anywhere" She realised that she also had survived in harsh and impossible circumstances. She herself was resourceful. She had managed, time and time again, to find a way of going on. She had continued to learn and grow.

"I'm not bad" she thought. She meant it. She would not even harm this horrible rat, so why label herself as bad?

She felt her heart calming down, her breath moving more freely. She sat down once more and started watching the rat intently. She could feel her heart reach out to God and it was not lost in space, she felt the connection, her heart warming up through it. She felt the answer come to her, blossoming from her heart: "There is no such thing as perfection. There is good and bad and all the shades in between. Colour is what gives our surroundings and nature beauty and life. What makes people beautiful and interesting is also their multi-coloured, multi-dimensional, kaleidoscope like personalities. If everything was pure white, there would be no distinction, no trees and ocean depths, no beauty, no colourful flowers or birds. If there was no shadow, all would be two dimensional, superficial, like a child's drawing on paper. Life is light and shadow and dark and shades. We love the shades of a tree, we love to sit in its shade, but we try to throw away our own depths, our own shadow, trying to hide it, shunning it, squashing it, hating it, fearing it. Beauty can be found in different shades. The beauty of a person manifests as much in their shadow as it does in their light."

She felt reassurance within herself, an understanding whispering into her heart: "You are not perfect Cara and that is what makes you so beautifully human and unique. Love your own shadow as you love the shadows played out in nature."

"God has a mournful face as well as a light one. How can you love and serve and be whole, if you try to deny the existence of half your nature. How can you accept others with compassion if you cannot accept yourself?"

"You think your destructive thoughts protect you from harm, but they shut you in, they cut half of your being out. Stop trying to control the rats, stop trying to kill them, accept them, watch them. Love your shadow. Only then can you truly love all."

"You have travelled far, you have suffered and smiled. You have survived. Now lift your head and embrace who you are fully. Love each step you take and you can then love where each of those steps lead you."

"Let go of those deeply rooted thoughts that deny your own worth, your right to exist and be, to live and love. Those are your mother's denial of you, let her keep them, they are not yours. Walk on, accepting and embracing your whole being as it is, with love."

"You exist, not for your mother, but as you are, for who you are, here on earth. You won't gain your mother's recognition by wiping yourself out of existence. You cannot suceed in that anyway. Have confidence in the space you inhabit. It is yours and you have much to give. Open up to the world, so that you can receive and give whole heartedly."

"Love yourself Cara, as you are"

She felt a glow light up within her and noticed the sun warming her face. She imagined herself shining in the sunlight and smiled. "Thank you" she thought. She saw herself as this tiny little lost figure in infinite wasteland, so isolated and alone.

And then she saw this little figure light up, shining, her glow reaching outwards, warming the wasteland and transforming it into colourful, lush forests, with streams flowing, birds singing and butterflies flying around like colourful stars shining bright in a black sky, like red poppies standing tall in endless greens.

She smiled. "I'm ready" she thought. She looked over at the rat, now standing still, paws held together in front of it, standing on its hind legs, watching her intently. "Thank you and God bless" she said to the rat and turned around. She was ready to leave the wastelands.

Cara found herself on soft sand once more. The sand was dark rather than golden. Black sand, as if the earth had been burned long ago and changed colour forever.

She could see huge waves roaring in and out of the shore. She wanted to be a part of them once more. She did not want to swim, or even move. She wanted to let go into their force and drift with them into the soft sand. The cold water beckoned her. She was not afraid of the strength of the waves. She did not feel afraid of drowning.

She walked out a short distance into the water. A large wave came crushing down on her and she was lost in water, in turmoil, for probably not more than a few seconds, but to her it felt like much longer. She could not breathe and struggle as she did, she was not able to surface for breath. She realised she was drowning. Then the wave rushed past her and she stood up. She was standing in water not much higher than her knees, yet seconds ago she had been drowning, water covering her head. She marvelled at the pure strength, will and force of water.

She looked out towards the ocean, waiting for the next wave, watching the ripples, the smaller waves, the rhythm of the sea. Then she saw it, a huge, roaring, crashing force of grey and white foam, rushing towards her. She stood her ground. Just as the wave reached her, an undercurrent tore her feet away from the ground. She was forced down under water by the force of the wave. The undercurrent was dragging her out, she fought in vain, she could not refind her footing. Her arms were beating powerless against the might of the ocean, her ears deafened by the roar, her throat and lungs full of salty water.

She resurfaced spluttering. She had not won, the wave

had lost interest in her and continued on, with speed and determination. She struggled back to the beach and sat down, too tired to move. She gazed out at the ocean, watching the waves rush in and out, lost in the commotion, in their fury. She was mesmerised, she could not look away, she had no desire to leave, she wanted to go back in.

She recovered her strength and ease in breathing and got up once more. She took a few strides into the water and waited. Wave after wave reached her, some reaching up to her head, but she was not yet deep enough to be lost in them. She felt their force, she felt air and life get knocked out of her as they surged and crashed against her chest. She liked the feeling. She turned her back on the waves and felt their strength crashing on her back, the foam tingling against her skin. Her whole body, her hair, inside her nose, every part of her, was soaking wet and salty. She could feel grains of sand clinging on to her wet skin.

She turned around and walked a few more steps, deeper into the ocean. The next wave caught her, pushing her down and sucking her back. This time she let go. It was so easy. Her legs hit the bottom of the ocean, she was rocked sideways, her legs getting sucked back behind her. She allowed the wave to have its way and held her breath. Eventually the wave left her like all the others and she was thrust up for air. It had moved her further away from land. She started to swim towards the sand, but the water was too powerful for her. She was moving further outward no matter how much effort and strength she put into her swimming. She felt fatigued. "I give up" she thought, "take me, you can have me". She continued to drift further out, waves crashing over her head, choking her breath. She was swallowing too much water. Once more she thought she would drown.

She could see the water rushing in, roaring, in a frenzy. She tried swimming again, but it was useless. As another wave approached she jumped up and flung herself into its foams. The crest of the wave threw her crashing towards the beach. Cara had found the way. She continued jumping into oncoming waves and riding them towards the safety of land until she was close enough to walk, forcing her legs to move against the undercurrent.

She flung herself on the beach, tired to breaking point, but feeling content, victorious against the mighty ocean. She had won the battle. She had won by surrendering, by letting go into the force of the waves, by letting them push her down to the ocean floor. She had reached safety by finding a way of working with them, so that they would carry her back to land, releasing herself to their will, power, energy and rhythm. Struggling and fighting against them had been futile. Surrendering to their might and power had saved her.

The trees in the clouds

She felt she was nearing the end of her journey. The air had changed once again. It was less salty, more fresh. She saw trees ahead and hastened her steps, excited to be near a forest, looking forward to hearing the ripple of leaves in the wind, hearing bird song and seeing flowers and fruit and butterflies.

As soon as she entered the forest, she was taken over by a sense of awe. The forest itself felt like an aspect of the Divine.

A sense of magic prevailed all around her. There was a stillness to this place she had not experienced even in the desert, where no living creature roamed, even in the dead of the night. Somehow the forest was alive, and yet still, lively, yet muted, without losing any of its vigour. Silence and stillness everywhere, but it was deeper than that. As if any sound made was transformed to a deeper dimension, somewhere else where sound had a different purpose. It wasn't that there was nothing around to make a sound, it was as if the sound was not perceptible to her ear, muted out of her three dimensional existence.

But then, she was not sure what would have made a sound anyway. There was no wind or breeze to rustle the trees and leaves, no birds singing, no animals wandering or grazing.

"What about my own foot steps?" she thought. Surely normally they would make a sound. The sound of crunching leaves, steps on earth, bracken breaking, stones moving. What about the rustling of my clothes or my hair? She moved fiercely trying to wake her surroundings up, trying to break the silence. No, nothing. Not a murmur. Nothing.

She wondered if she ought to feel afraid. Or excited. Or something. No, she wasn't afraid. She was curious maybe, interested, but even that feeling was mild. It didn't matter. Nothing seemed to really matter in this place of muted magic.

She didn't really care why there was no sound, no other being around, seemingly no other form of life.

As she gazed at them she felt that even the trees weren't quite alive. Apart from the lack of movement and sound, there was a lack of green. Or of any colour that gave the impression of life. Their brown trunks hanging down from fluffy, thick, endlessly deep clouds. A mist everywhere. The mist and the clouds were like leaves a and growth around the trees.

"It's all brown, grey and white" she thought. No other colours. And as she continued to gaze around she felt more and more that she had been mistaken. She could not see any brown. The trees were all different shades of grey. The mist surrounding them also grey, but a lighter shade.

"No, the brown's different. The brown's where life is" she decided.

Then she saw the shadows. Yes, relief. The forest had shadow, so it must be alive. There were varied depths to the light and the shade. She knew she had reached her destination for now. She needed to be in the shadow. Watch it, feel it, be it, hear it, smell it. In such silence shadow could be heard.

She touched the bark of a tree, the one nearest to her. It wasn't rough as she had expected. In fact her hand seemed to glide over it. She could not feel any friction. Smooth, yet somehow not really smooth at the same time.

It was then she felt It's presence. Like a universal presence, one that had no beginning, no end, no middle. One that had no time and took up no space, had no location, centre, or circumferance. One that just was. She remembered how It had told her "I am". Nothing else could have possibly mattered then. Nothing else mattered now.

She had always imagined she would feel God's presence as love maybe or something vast with a particular message or a sound. What she felt was so much simpler: "I am". God is everything, everywhere and beyond. God is timeless and placeless. God is. And that was the strongest, most powerful message of all. Having felt that, she knew nothing else could possibly matter, ever again. God isn't just love or wisdom, God is beyond those too. Even universal love could not describe God, because God contains that, yet everything more than that as well. We don't need to understand, see or feel God in one way or another. God simply is.

Shadow and light as one, together

She was lying on her back, gazing at a black sky. "A whole universe lies out there", she thought. Stars sparkling everywhere, millions of them. Each one home to different lives, wisdoms and joys. They twinkled with so much playfulness and good nature, she felt as if they were communicating with her directly, inviting her to join in their fun, welcoming her into their midst.

She could feel her back on cold, solid ground. Earth, the nourishing, nurturing, supporting mother, nothing like that devouring dragon, or the poisonous droplets, or gnawing rats. Vegetation grew out of the earth, soil held seeds and nourished them until they were ready to sprout out into light. She felt safe feeling its cold secure solidity beneath her. Earth, mother nature, the universal mother had held her in her dark, cool embrace for as long as had been necessary. Within that embrace and darkness Cara had grown from a lost seed into a blossoming flower. Now she had been released back out into the universe, into light. She could feel her roots in solid ground and her arms reaching up into lightness and sky.

She no longer feared darkness. She was no longer afraid of getting lost, taking a wrong turn, ending up in a wrong place. All places belong to God, all places lead to God, they all hold learning and growth, they are all good as well as bad, they all have lessons to teach, shelters to provide, wisdom to pass on and peace to share. It didn't really matter where life led her. She felt secure in her belief that life and the universe knew what was best for her and as long as she flowed with them, she would be okay.

She no longer worried about the next day, or the next moment even. Now, this moment, the very moment she was in, was all that mattered. And now she was at peace. Then again, since she'd stopped worrying about the next moment, she had felt a sense of peace within her the whole time. "God is timeless", she thought, this moment, the now, spreading out forever, encompassing the past, the present and the future.

She no longer thought about the past. It had come and gone. The wounds, the lessons and the gifts remained, but they were part of her being now. They no longer jarred against her. They no longer felt sharp or hard. They no longer called for a fight. They no longer stabbed her chest and drew blood, or suffocated her lungs. They no longer speeded up her heart until it might explode, or stopped her breath and stilled all movement and life within her, numbing all desire to move forward. They were subtly there in the background, part of her skin and bones, but they formed a wiser, more mature, more accepting part of her. And what was real, what continued with each breath, were the gifts of the wounds, the lessons, the understanding, the wisdom. The gifts were what lived on within her, not the pain or the heartache she had felt at times. Those things belonged to those times and those times had passed.

She felt at peace there, with the solid ground, the sparkling stars, the unknown and the calm, serenity she felt in her heart.

The rising sun

She woke up with the gradual appearance of the sun. Clouds hid the sun from view, but the light it was emitting could not be held back or hidden behind the clouds. They broke through, lighting the sky up with scarlet, orange, red, pink, yellow and many shades and combinations more. It was a glorious sight. The clouds, that could have been dark, restricting, hiding the light, instead had turned into a rainbow of colours and shades. The sky was lit up like a mystical fire, like a fairytale image, surreal, intangible, yet real in front of her eyes.

Her heart stirred, lit up by such glorious beauty. "Shadow and light" she thought, "the source of light, the source of darkness and this kaleidoscope of vivid colours, bright, joyful, energetic, sublime".

Nature held within it light and shadow both, simultaneously, everywhere. Accepting shadow in the world, within yourself, in others, accepting with love and holding the shadow up with the light, not hiding it, burying it, shunning it, these were what had brought her inner peace and true acceptance.

The world seemed to open up to her. Suddenly there was potential, a myriad of possibilities, excitement to be found and a full life to be led. How far she had come from the stale, rotting feeling of her past. She could smell roses, overflowing with sweetness. And she could feel a breeze. It was so gentle, it felt more like a caress against her skin. The wind was kissing her face, its lips moist with droplets of water, mingling with the tears in her eyes. She was deeply touched, not sad, she felt happy. Her happiness was rising and flowing from somewhere deep within her. It was not a superficial momentary happiness that lands from outside, flickers and dies out. It was a happiness she felt in the warm serenity of her heart.

All around her she could see beauty. She could hear it, feel it, sense it, breathe it in. Everything looked so extraordinary to her eyes, so unique, so colourful and so extravagant in their riches.

She turned her glance inwards and noticed that even her memories seemed beautiful through her new found sight. They did not bore into her with their dark weight, nor were they totally clear, pure or clean. They were vibrantly colourful and full of depth. They had shades, presents from the shadow, from the darker side of the soul. Just like the glorious colours spreading over the sky were gifts from the clouds. The shadow, the part of us we try to disown, ignore, squash down, avoid, deny. The side of us that is just as real and alive as the light, that can guide us just as much and teach us even more. It is also the side of us that we are afraid to touch. Are we afraid we'll be taken over by the darkness? But how can darkness take over if we bring light to shine on it, to make it visible? It can only wrap us up completely if we bury it in deeper darkness, where it can grow and spread. As soon as we bring it out, see it and accept it, we are shining the light of our soul, of our heart and the soul of the universe on it. It can no longer lie buried. Its corners are transformed into plays of light and shadow, at times sparkling, at times cosily dark, at times brightening. Play of light and shadow, depth and surface, shades of colour, depths of colour, of beauty, of life.

It is the combination of light and shadow, the play of light on shadow and shadow on light that gives the world and all on it their beauty. Can you imagine a pure, blank screen? Two dimensional because of lack of shadow, colourless to keep it pure white. How boring, how lacking in life, beauty, image, character. How pointless. Where's the beauty in pure blank white? An initially blank canvas grows in beauty and meaning as colour is added. Colours of different shades, figures with shadow to make them stand out, to bring life into them, make them three dimensional. It is colour that attracts. A blank canvas says nothing, moves no one. Once it is full of contradictions, images, colours, figures, only then does it have beauty, only then can you comment on it and what it means, only then can you love it.

If God is all and God includes all, so then by definition God must include shadow also. If God is all, then God must hold good and bad, light and dark, happy and sad, joy and suffering. We are told that God loves all and forgives all, yet we refuse to love everyone and forgive ourselves or others. If everything and everyone is part of a greater whole, a small reflection of all in the universe, should we not accept and love all, including ourselves, without judgement or hatred?

Why is it so hard for us to accept our own shadow and to own it? Why do we either act as if it doesn't exist, turn our eyes away from it, close our beings to its existence, or if by some push of fate we're forced to see it, acknowledge its existence, do we then shun it, try to bury it, try to change it, kill it or throw it away?

What we do in the process is drive it down deeper underground and we end up splitting our own souls. We deny ourselves the richness of our being, we rob ourselves of colour and play, we drive ourselves to contempt and self-hatred, self-abuse and self-denial.

There is relief and joy in acceptance. There is life and guidance in darkness. And the most valuable, beautiful being of all is not one that is made of pure light, but one that is whole, that holds within it both light and shadow and all the shades in between.

Lush greens

She came upon them quite suddenly. It seemed as though one minute she was standing in grey, brown, white shades, then, without any warning she was walking through lush green vegetation. She had never seen or even dreamed of so much vibrancy, so much energy bright with colour. Every shade of green, bursting with life and colour, so many different shades and variations. Great big plants, green from the earth to their tops. Big leaves thrusting out, brimming with life, seeking the sun. Brown trunks covered with moss, small leaves scattered all over them. Stunning large broad leaves, glistening with dew. Light greens and dark greens, greens mixed with red and auburn, greens mixed with blue. Glittering water droplets, shining golden rays.

A cool breeze was playing on her cheeks and the air felt moist, rich with rain drops held in mid air. She touched a leaf, then another. She wanted to take it all in, breathe their grassy scent, lie in the overgrowth, feel their rich texture, inhale the scent of life emanating from them.

There was so much vibrant colour around her, her senses were filled to the brim. She thought she might overflow. Dark red leaves, white blossoms, pink flowers, lilac shoots, golden petals, deep red blossoms, all competing with each other, expressing their joy for life, playful in the early morning air.

And then the skies opened. A waterfall from above, dense, fast raindrops clambering down, all in a race to reach the earth. She lifted her face up to heaven, feeling the water stream down her eyelids and cheeks, feeling herself getting wet, grateful for the touch of water, grateful for its life giving purity.

The rain was like a friendly monster, gentle with its touch, yet loud, broadcasting its strength and freedom. The sense of freedom that came with the raindrops filled Cara's soul.

She opened her arms wide, smiling up to the sky and started dancing, turning, laughing with joy. She felt pure and innocent, full of life and love. She was laughing hard now, a well of happiness growing within her and overflowing outwards. She wondered if she'd explode from sheer happiness, it was all so much, her whole body vibrant, filled with a dancer's poise and strength. Her muscles felt alive, as they kicked into action. She felt so light, as if she was flying, unencumbered by weight and the pull of gravity, free even from the forces of nature.

She danced and ran in the rain until it slowed down gradually, diminishing into gentle small droplets, scattered and light. She gathered her skirt, wringing out the water, still laughing inwardly. She continued to move through the trees, feeling happy and light. She did not care at all where she went, as long as she was wandering in this glorious, vibrant, life giving place. Nothing else mattered.

Cara's progress over the next few days was slow. She felt so good, her body felt strong, her heart full and vibrant, her eyes skipped around, landing on delightful vision after delightful vision. She was in no hurry. She wanted to drink it all in, fill her whole body and soul with beauty. Her surroundings were beautiful and she moved through them slowly, watching, gazing, touching, breathing, letting the beauty, peace and joy emanating from every plant and stone around her nourish her very being.

Presently she arrived at a stream. It was flowing peacefully between its two banks, Cara sat down to enjoy it for a while. She listened to the playful chatter of the stream. The stream was laughing, chuckling, a sound mirroring what she felt within her.

The stream skipped and danced, singing and joyful, tumbling over stones in the stream bed. Flowers grew either side of it, butterflies dancing between them. The whole area was bright with vibrant colour, hundreds of shades of greens, reds, oranges, purples, blues, browns. Cara felt her soul fill to the brim with awe and beauty. She felt herself glow, mirroring the beauty surrounding her. She decided to make her home here, at least for a while.

She walked along the stream, moving towards its source, looking for shelter, somewhere she could set up a temporary home. She found the perfect place in the midst of a gathering of trees. They were so rich with leaves on their branches, growing close together, that they created a tent like structure, into which she entered. She cleared the earth using branches and bracken and piled leaves in a corner for her bed. Then she walked over to the entrance of her new home and sat there watching the stream, the butterflies, birds and leaping fish. She felt she could stay there forever and never need anything else from the world. She had found her paradise.

The next few months went by in peace. Cara spent her time walking, bathing, watching, listening, thinking and feeling. She set up a corner for reflection in her shelter, which she created by placing pretty stones and shells on a long, flat piece of wood. She placed a fresh flower on the shelf every morning and said her prayers of gratitude. The sense of peace grew within her and she found herself settling in with a clear conscience and a light heart.

Her dreams were of her surroundings, of the pretty stream, the butterflies and flowers, the trees and the sky. She dreamed of journeys, of love and loss, of beauty and faith.

One night as she slept the image of her loved one returned to her. He was riding off into the distance. There was a sense of heaviness about him, as if he was carrying a heavy burden. His horse was moving slowly, as if it too felt the weight of the burden its rider was carrying. Cara felt sorry for him. She wished the stranger light and love. She woke up to realise he did not bring pain or anguish to her heart any longer. She remembered him with a sense of poignancy, as something once had, deeply felt, cherished and lost. She got up and sat by the stream. "I release you" she said to her rider, "I release you into the gentle, playful dance of the stream. Go well, be light. Goodbye"